KU-714-961

GEORGIA LE CARRE

Author's Note

BEAUTY AND THE DARK
is a standalone erotic romance with no
cliffie and a guaranteed HEA. It contains
mature themes, strong language, and
steamy situations. All characters are 18+
years of age and all sexual acts are
consensual.

:-)

Don't forget to look out for the sneak
peak of my next book...

THE BLIND READER

Enjoy!

ALSO BY GEORGIA

The Billionaire Banker Series

Owned
42 Days
Besotted
Seduce Me
Love's Sacrifice

Masquerade

Pretty Wicked (novella)

Disfigured Love

Hypnotized

Crystal Jake

Sexy Beast

Wounded Beast

Beautiful Beast

Dirty Aristocrat

You Don't Own Me 1 & 2

The Bad Boy Wants Me

You Don't Know Me

Click on the link below to receive news of my latest releases and exclusive content.

http://bit.ly/1oe9WdE

Editors: Caryl Milton, Elizabeth Burns & IS Creations
Cover Designer:
http://www.ctcovercreations.com/
Photographer:
https://www.facebook.com/DKArtistics/?pnref=lhc
Model:
https://www.facebook.com/kimberleighmichellemodel/
?pnref=lhc
Proofreader: http:// http://nicolarheadediting.com/

BEAUTY AND THE DARK

Published by Georgia Le Carre
Copyright © 2016 by Georgia Le Carre

The right of Georgia Le Carre to be identified as the
Author of the Work has been asserted by her in
accordance with the copyright, designs and patent act
1988.
All rights reserved. No part of this publication may be
reproduced, stored in a retrieval system, or transmitted,
in any form or by any means without the prior written
permission of the publisher, nor be otherwise circulated
in any form of binding or cover other than that which it
is published and without a similar condition being
imposed on the subsequent purchaser.
All characters in this publication are fictitious, any
resemblance to real persons, living or dead, is purely
coincidental.
ISBN: 9781910575-45-1

You can discover more information about Georgia Le
Carre and future releases here.
https://www.facebook.com/georgia.lecarre
https://twitter.com/georgiaLeCarre
http://www.goodreads.com/GeorgiaLeCarre

Appreciations

I wish to extend my deepest and most profound gratitude to:

Caryl Milton
Elizabeth Burns
Nicola Rhead
Tracy Gray
Brittany Urbaniak

Prologue

Jack

(Five Years Previously)

https://www.youtube.com/watch?v=vt1Pwfnh5pc
(Hurt)

"**G**et up, Englishman," a harsh voice barks at the same time the butt of an AK47 jams into my solar plexus.

My eyes fly open as I jack- knife upwards, winded and stunned. My hands flail wildly as I attempt to grab the thing that slammed into me, but the man has withdrawn it. He is looking down at me contemptuously, his smooth face gleaming with sweat. I get up on my elbows and take gasping breaths of air, but the air is so thick and hot it's like

sucking lava into your lungs.
Malevolent.

"Get up," the man yells again, and roughly pushes the barrel of his semi-automatic into my chest, driving me onto my back.

"What the fuck," I swear, furious now. "If you want me to get up, quit fucking pushing me back on the bed."

He moves back and I swing my legs down, my booted feet hitting the mud floor with a thud. I went to bed drunk, and my head is banging like some prick on crack is working an industrial sledgehammer inside it. I wince with the pain. Damn, they had to pick tonight of all nights.

Gritting my teeth, I force my head up.

The tent flap has been left open and the outside camp light seeps in allowing me a good look at the men. There are two of them and they are dressed in army gear, but it is clear they are rebels.

The one standing closest to me is of medium height, muscular, and as dark as the African night. Sweat is running down his temple in rivulets. He is wearing his ammunition belt as if it is a glinting scarf around his shoulders. His eyes tell me he is battle hardened and trigger-happy.

This is one man you don't want to piss off.

The other man is standing by the tent flap with his gun held loosely at his side. He is tall and lean and wearing a maroon cap with badges on it. His army jacket is unbuttoned and underneath he is wearing a badly stained white T-shirt. There is something infinitely more dangerous about him than the jacked up, muscle shirt in front of me.

"You get up now. Come with us," Beefy commands.

"Fuck you," I tell him.

He raises his gun and points it directly at me.

I start laughing. At first lightly, then more raucously.

"Shut up, Englishman, or I kill you," he shouts, bringing the black hole of his weapon closer to my face, but already, I can see that I have confused him. He has never encountered a man laughing at the thought of his own violent death.

It infuriates him that I am not afraid of him. "Stop laughing," he screams.

I stop laughing, grab the barrel of his semi with both hands and pull it tight against my forehead. They say your whole life, everything you've ever done, all the people you've hurt and loved, flash before your eyes as you exit this cruel earth. Well, not for me.

I feel nothing.

Just numbness.

"Fucking do it! Shoot me," I dare, staring him in the eye. "You'd be doing me a favor.'

"This man is crazy," he pronounces, turning dumbfounded to his comrade.

The dangerous one steps closer. His hat was covering his eyes so I couldn't see them before. Now I do. They're chillingly empty. Without a hint of humanity. He comes right up to my bed and stares down at me curiously.

Well, fuck you too. If he's looking to see terror in my face, he won't. Only darkness.

"You have a death wish, Englishman? How ironic then that you have come here to save people from death,' he says in perfect English.

Obviously, he didn't pick up that upper-class accent in Africa. He must have been educated in England. He's right though. Even I can see the unintended irony.

"What do you want from me?" I ask.

'Our leader has been shot. You are a doctor. You can save him.'

'Thanks for the offer, but I think I'll pass. Your leader is a fucking mass murderer.'

He smiles. 'We are reasonable people, Englishman. We will give you a choice. Come with us or we will behead every man, woman, and child in this village and you can stay and bury them."

A bead of sweat trickles down my spine. That's the problem with this oppressive heat. You go to sleep sweaty, you wake up sweaty, and you get out of the shower sweaty. I look at the doorway to my tent. Through the open flap hordes of mosquitoes are flying in. There'll be no sleep tonight.

"Where was he shot?"

Beefy points to his abdomen. "Here."

"When did it happen?'

"Yesterday, at noon."

That's a long time to be injured in this climate. Mud, dirt, bacteria, and little insects love an open wound: all safe and warm and filled with delicious food.

"How far away are you?"

"Three hour's drive."

'It's been more than twenty-four hours. Even if I treat him he may not survive, I tell them.'

'No, our leader is strong and you will save him,' Mr. Muscle declares confidently.

I sigh. "Yeah, I'll come, but I'll need a drink first."

One

Sofia

"Do roses know their thorns can hurt?" – a quote attributed to JonBenét Ramsey from Lawrence Schiller's *Perfect Murder, Perfect Town*

"**B**ut you promised," my sister accuses, eyeing me with frustration.

I bend my head to hide my face with my hair. "I know I promised, but I can't, Lena. Not just yet. Not this Christmas. Maybe next year." My voice is low, ashamed, and guilty.

"Look at me, Sofia," Lena demands.

I raise my head. She is staring at me with tears in her beautiful eyes. My sister used to be a world famous model until she gave it all up to get married and have little Irina. If you meet her on the street, you'll never imagine that we are sisters. She is tall with long blonde hair and piercingly blue eyes, and I am small, with sandy brown hair and chocolate eyes. She inherited her height and coloring from my father, and I got mine from my mother.

I lift my hand and wipe away the solitary tear rolling down her lovely cheek. "Please don't cry, Lena," I plead. "I'm just not ready. I can't do it yet. One day I will, but not right now."

"It's been a year," she whispers. "You have to make an effort, Sofia. At some point you're going to have to climb out of this dull, solitary existence you have crawled into and start living again. There is beauty out there."

I sigh sadly. My sister wants me to forget. To move on. To be happy. She doesn't know what I have been through. I have not even told her a third of what happened to me.

"I *am* living and there is beauty around me," I murmur. "I love you, and Irina, and Guy, and the dogs. I go for

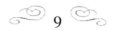

walks. I paint. I play the piano. Just because I don't want to go to this party doesn't mean I don't have a life."

She looks at me steadily. "You *never* go out, or meet people. You are as silent as a shadow, and if no one addresses you directly you would never talk to anyone, would you?"

I drop my eyes. It's true. I don't want to go out, meet people, or even speak to anyone. My experiences with people have taught me that they are immeasurably cruel, deceitful, and disloyal. I don't trust them. If at all possible I want to live here quietly with my sister and never venture outside the vast grounds of this remote and wonderful castle.

"I talk to the dogs," I say with a smile, but my attempt to lighten the mood has no effect on her.

"Please come," she begs. "For me."

I frown. I'd give up my life for my sister, I hate to let her down, but even the thought of going to a party makes my body tremble. "I'd only spoil the party for everyone else," I tell her.

It's the wrong thing to say. Her back grows ramrod straight and her eyes sparkle with steely determination. I am older than her, but anybody looking at us will think that I am the younger one. She seems so much stronger and more powerful.

"No, you won't," she says firmly. "You'll never leave my side. Guy and I will take care of you the whole time."

I swallow the lump rising in my throat. "Oh, Lena. It's a Christmas Eve party. You don't want to be worrying about me the whole time. You should go out and have fun with Guy." I smile brightly. "I'll stay here and take care of Irina. Make sure she doesn't get into any mischief."

She crosses her arms in front of her chest. Oh, God! I hate it when she does that. It means it will be impossible to sway her from her purpose.

"Thank you. That is very kind of you, but Irina already has a babysitter lined up."

"Surely she'll prefer me to take care of her."

"Irina will be asleep by eight-thirty. You're getting into your new red dress and coming with me," she says firmly.

'I can't wear the red dress. It's too obvious."

"Fine. Wear the black velvet one. You look stunning in it."

Cornered, I try to find other avenues of escape. "I don't even know the people who are throwing the party."

She senses victory and grins. "The Barringtons? You'll love them. Well, at least you'll love Lana. Her husband, Blake, is a bit reserved and hard to know, but underneath the unapproachable exterior he has a heart of gold." Her eyes light up. "Besides, if we go early you can meet their kids. They're gorgeous. The boy is so cute you'll want to pop him between two slices of bread and eat him."

I smile. I know she is talking about the children because she knows they are the only humans I can bear to talk to. "What's his name?"

"Sorab."

"That's an unusual name."

"Yeah. Apparently it's an old Persian name. His mother is a quarter Persian."

"It sounds almost Russian."

She smiles broadly. "A bit. So you'll come?"

"All right, but I don't want to stay long. Maybe the driver can bring me back early."

She shakes her head decisively. "Guy and me don't plan to stay long either. You'll go with us and you'll come back with us."

I nod reluctantly. "Okay."

She stands and, pulling me up, whirls me around the way we used to when we were children living in a tiny wooden house at the edge of a Russian forest.

"Thank you, my darling sister," she says and kisses my cheek. "You're the only family I have left and I want you to be happy."

"I am happy," I say automatically, but the truth is I don't know what happiness means.

When we were young we were always terrified of my father. After he sold me to those men I stopped being a person, I became a piece of meat with a name. *Open your legs, Sofia. Wider, Sofia. Wider still, Sofia.* Until I began to hate the sound of my name. I shudder at the painful memories.

My sister puts the palms of her hands on either side of my cheeks. "One day …" she lets the whisper filled with promise and hope trail away.

Two

Sofia

As it happens we don't go early, and by the time we get into London it is already 9.30pm. We walk up the black and white stone path to the doorway of a large white house.

Flakes of snow swirl down from a black sky and land on my nose and cheeks. My stomach is in a tight knot and my hands are clammy with sweat. I run them nervously down my cream coat. As we arrive at the front door, Lena turns her head and looks at me.

"Are you alright?"

I nod stiffly.

"Just relax. It's only a small group of really nice people. We're just going to have a couple of drinks then we'll leave. It'll be fun, you'll see."

I nod again.

Guy touches my arm and I turn blindly towards him. I love Guy almost as deeply as I love my sister. I think I've loved him from the moment I laid eyes on him. He is the kindest man on earth.

What he did for me I will never be able to repay. Until today only Guy knows what I was when he found me in that godforsaken brothel. You cannot imagine the darkness of my existence, how low and degraded I was. I had been repeatedly raped, beaten, locked up, forced to have sex with so many men that I no longer had a will of my own. I was so traumatized I was barely human. I cowered in fear. My will was Valdislav's. If he asked me to do something I would have done it no matter how depraved or disgusting.

I stared blankly at Guy when I heard him tell Valdislav he wanted to buy me not just for the night, or for the week, but actually take me away from there. I could see that he was in awe of Guy. I could see instantly that Guy was different. He radiated power and the confidence that comes from immense wealth.

Valdislav sniggered. "I'm going to do you a favor. She's lazy. Pick another girl."

"I don't want another. This is the one I want," Guy replied.

The men stared at each other until Valdislav frowned. He wanted to make a sale to the rich man, but he didn't want to let me go. Even though he had a whole harem of women, most of them far better looking than me, I was his favorite. No matter how many women he slept with, the sadist always came back to torture me. His greatest pleasure came from making me submit to his sick desires.

"No, not this one," Valdislav said, his eyes flashing. "This one is mine."

However, that day Guy put so much cash on the table, more than Valdislav had ever seen, more than he could ever hope to earn in his lifetime, that he

couldn't refuse. Not for a piece of meat, anyway. Guy walked over to me. While he was negotiating with Valdislav his eyes had been so cold and hard I was terrified of my new owner, but bending his head, he whispered, "I'm taking you back to Lena."

The shock was unbelievable. I never thought. I did not even dare to dream such a thing. My legs gave way beneath me and the world went black. Later I found out that he had to carry me to the car waiting outside.

When I woke up I was in a beautiful room. Guy was sitting on a chair next to the bed.

"Where is Lena?" I whispered.

"You are not ready to see her. Heal first. Then you can see her."

I grasped the bed covers tightly and fought back the tears. I was sure he had tricked me. "Where is she?"

"She is in London."

He did not seem to be lying. "Does she know I'm here?"

"Not yet."

"Why not?"

"Because I love her and I don't want to break her heart by letting her see you in this state."

I stared at him in shock. What a wonderful man. He wanted to spare her the pain. Suddenly, shame flooded into me. Lena was clean. I was not. I squeezed my eyes shut. "Don't tell her I'm here. I can't face her. I'm dirty. I'm too dirty," I began to sob.

He leaned forward, his eyes blazing with inner fury. 'You're not dirty. You're an angel with a broken wing, but broken things can heal. You will fly again. I will make you fly," he grated.

I couldn't reply because I was crying so much.

He was as good as his word. Immediately, he set about calling in an army of doctors, nurses and professionals to heal me. When the haze brought about by the drugs left my system and my head cleared, I just wanted to die. I couldn't cope with the things I had done.

All those men.

All those filthy things.

Until then I had been in survival mode. Knowing nothing but the irresistible urge to survive. Feelings are a luxury. I felt nothing even at the worst kind of humiliation and degradation.

The first feelings I experienced were rage. Terrible fury. It boiled and bubbled like lava in my blood. It ate me up. I trembled with it. I lashed out. I wailed. I screamed. I sobbed for hours. I was filled with hate. I hated my father. I hated my mother even more for what she allowed my father to do to me.

I hated Valdislav.

I hated myself.

I hated the world.

I hated God.

I even hated my blameless sister. It was not enough that she was beautiful, she had found a wonderful man like

Guy. I turned my hatred to Guy. I screamed hysterically at him.

Naturally, I hated the people who had been brought to cure me. I tried to claw my psychiatrist's face and had to be held back by the servants. She pissed me off. Sitting there as smug as a well-fed cat spouting glib nonsense.

"But how do *you* feel about it?"

"I feel like scratching your fucking face to shreds."

All the professionals were in agreement. I was too damaged for outpatient treatment. In fact, in their professional opinion, I was more than a little mad. I should be locked up and medicated. Guy wasted no time.

He fired them all and did a strange thing.

He went to Tibet to personally call on a powerful shaman to come to the castle and take over my rehabilitation. I don't think money changed hands. It was a special favor.

Master Yeshe was only as tall as me. I still remember the day he arrived. I was curled up tight on the bed. My thumb was in my mouth and I was sucking it so hard my thumb was red and raw. I was not angry that day. My mind was numb, but tears were pouring from my eyes. My body was remembering some great hurt.

Dressed in blue robes he walked towards the bed with the help of a crooked black walking stick. I couldn't see him through the haze of tears. I could only tell that he had a sparse white beard, and his eyes were so small they were merely slits in his round, ageless face. He came very close to my body and held his forefinger six inches in front of me.

Suddenly, the tears stopped. I stared at him in shock.

He smiled. "You will be well again," he said in Russian.

His method of dealing with my uncontrollable fits of rage and pain was bizarre, but it worked.

Every day for three weeks we met before the sun came up in the foyer, which was filled with the scent of lilies. On the first day, I tried to wish him good morning, but he touched his finger to his lips and pointed to his feet. They were bare. I took my shoes off, and without exchanging a single word, we began our walk.

We walked barefoot through the vast grounds of the castle. We never spoke. Not one word. The ground was so cold the soles of my feet turned blue, and a few times I hurt myself on thorns and sharp stones, but always at the end of the walk I felt good. The soles of my feet became toughened and, slowly, every day I felt a little better than I had the day before. The demons were leaving me.

I was healing!

I began to accept all those terrible, unfair things had happened to me even though I had done nothing to deserve them. Valdislav could never again come near me, tell me what to do, or touch me. In this safe setting I would slowly rebuild my life. Become a different person. I learned to be grateful that I had another chance. Another chance to be peaceful, and for the first time in my life to be master of my own body. I started to look forward to my sister's arrival.

On the day Master Yeshe left the castle he said his last words to me. I remember them even now. He was drinking butter tea.

"Baby steps."

As he uttered those words, he moved his hands as if they were feet taking small steps.

They were nothing words, but their power to me was and is incalculable. In every situation that looked like it could overwhelm me, I said those words

silently, and suddenly I was quietly walking barefoot with him in the cold morning air inhaling the smell of moss, rotting leaves, and wet earth. And just like that I was filled with peace and tranquility again.

Three

Sofia

Guy looks down at me from his great height, his eyes kind and protective. "We don't have to go in if you don't want to," he says gently.

Love and gratitude well up in my heart for him as I smile shakily.

"Don't tell her that," my sister tells Guy, her voice anxious. "She has to start somewhere. This is a safe environment for her. We've come this far. She can do it."

"Don't force her, Lena. There is no hurry."

I look from Guy to my sister. She is frowning and all kinds of thoughts and fears are visible on her face. She desperately wants me to agree to go in. For her this is an important milestone. My first social engagement after more than two years at the castle. All this time I have only ever gone out to the village to buy little bits and pieces.

She has my best interests at heart and I don't want to let her down, but my eyes glance longingly at the car waiting at the end of the path. In my head I hear Master Yeshe's voice.

"Baby steps."

I take a deep breath. I can do this. This is my life. I control it. Valdislav is a bad memory.

I force a smile on to my lips. "It's okay, Lena. We'll go in."

My sister's face breaks into a relieved smile. "Thank God. I promise you, Sofia you won't regret doing this.'

With an imperceptible nod, Guy puts his finger to the doorbell and the door is opened by a smiling, olive-skinned woman in a black dress. Her accent marks her as Spanish. She welcomes us into the warmth of the interior and closes the door.

The air is perfumed with the smell of cinnamon and spices. I can hear the laughter of people coming from deeper in the house.

I look around me curiously.

The tall, highly polished granite hallway looks festive and welcoming with its Christmas decorations, including a mini Santa's cabin in the woods tucked away in one corner. There is a plate of biscuits and a glass of milk outside the little door.

The sight makes me smile.

I knew Santa Claus did not exist from the time I was tiny. My father never made any attempt to infuse magic into our lives. How wonderful that the Barrington's children have so much.

A tall girl in a white shirt and black skirt comes into the hallway. She smiles at us and offers to take our coats. I watch Guy help Lena out of hers and give it to the girl before turning to me. I have an irrational desire to keep mine on a little longer, but I let him help me out of my coat. Instantly, I feel cold and horribly exposed. I fidget with my dress. It is pure white and beautifully cut, but I realize I probably shouldn't have worn it tonight. It is too revealing. The black dress would have been better.

'You look beautiful,' my sister whispers.

She means to be encouraging, but I shrink further into myself, utterly certain I won't be able to fit in. That old terror comes back in a rush. One of the men will recognize me. He will crack a rude joke about me. I will bring shame to Guy and my sister. My lungs suddenly feel empty and I draw in a shuddering breath. Both Guy and my sister's head whip around in my direction.

"Are you all right?" Lena asks. Her eyes are sharp with concern that she has pushed me to take this step too quickly.

I swallow hard.

Baby steps.

It is crazy to think that the rough and ready men who came to Valdislav's

brothel would be invited to such a fine house. Even the idea is stupid. Of course, I *can* do this. I straighten my spine. "Yes. Yes, I am," I say firmly.

"We can still go home if you want to," Guy offers.

I shake my head. In my mind I am walking barefoot in the woods amongst the yolk-yellow bulbs of winter aconites dotted on the frozen ground. Everything is still and calm. There is nothing to fear. No one can hurt me here. Not while Master Yeshe is around.

My sister and Guy take up position on either side of me. They have broken themselves up to offer me support. I silently vow not to let them down, or bring embarrassment to them tonight.

I'll simply smile and say hello to anyone who approaches me, then I'll find a quiet corner and sit down. Nobody will even know that I'm here. I'll make myself invisible. The sound of our shoes echo around the grand space as we follow the olive-skinned woman.

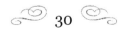

We are shown to a large, elegant room with a massive marble fireplace. There is a cheerful log fire burning in it. The mantelpiece is garlanded with greenery and decorated with white candles. Next to the fireplace there is a massive Christmas tree festooned with beaded snowballs, knit sweater ornaments, 'snow' branches, angels, pine cones and delicate glass balls. Lots of gaily wrapped presents are arranged under the tree.

I allow my gaze to quickly skim over the group. There are about fifteen to twenty people assembled in the room. The men are in dark suits and the women in party dresses. I try not to look at their faces.

A stunningly beautiful lady dressed in an elegant wraparound black dress comes forward. She has creamy skin and long black hair. "Merry Christmas," she greets, kissing Guy and Lena.

"Is this Sofia, then?" she asks with a warm smile.

"Merry Christmas to you too, Lana," my sister replies. "Yes, this is my sister Sofia. Sofia, this is Lana Barrington."

"Merry Christmas,' I echo, holding my clammy hand out.

Instead of shaking my hand, Lana grasps my shoulders and kisses me on both cheeks. 'How lovely to finally meet you. Your sister talks about you all the time and I've been dying to meet you ever since I heard that you walk barefoot on frozen ground," she gushes.

"Oh. I ... er ... it's ... lovely to meet you too," I stammer, and mentally kick myself for being so lame.

Her smile doesn't falter. "Well, come in and try a glass of mulled wine. It's made from a very special old Roman recipe. It has saffron, mastic, and roasted date stones."

As if on cue, a waitress stops by carrying a tray full of thick glasses three-quarters filled with a murky liquid the color of ox blood.

A tall, handsome man with cold, dismissive eyes comes up to us. His body language tells me immediately that he must be our host, the reserved husband, Blake Law Barrington. Lena says he used to be a banker to the bankers and that his wealth is quite literally astounding. One look at him and I believe it.

He shakes Guy's hand and exchanges greetings with him before turning to smile at Lena and me. As our gazes touch I have a strange sensation: this is a dangerous man. Underneath his beautifully cut, civilized clothes he has no limits. He could kill with a smile if he had to. I have met men like him before only once or twice. Their coldness reaches into their souls. He extends his hand and I slip mine into it. His handshake is firm, but impersonal.

He breaks our handshake, slips his arm around his wife's waist, and looks down at her. Instantly, I see that he adores her. She is the real love of his life.

Without her he would be a heartless monster.

Something tugs at my heart, a longing to be part of a great love, but I know I'll never let anyone get that close to me. My firm intention is to live and die alone.

Four

Sofia

My sister gently places her hand on my back and steers me towards the fireplace. I realize I am shivering. She positions me with the tree on my left and the fireplace on my right. I take a sip of my wine. It tastes sweet and smoky. I take another sip. And another.

Slowly the heat from the fireplace warms my back while I stand there silently, and listen to my sister talking to Lana. I notice that Lana has taken the cue from my sister and does not try to draw me into their conversation. The mulled wine seeps into my veins, warming and relaxing me.

No one approaches us and I begin to feel protected and hidden away amongst the greenery and tight circle made by my sister and Lana. My body loosens. My skin feels warm and glowing. This is not so bad. I can do this.

For the first time I notice the music playing discreetly in the background. I listen to the snatches of conversation floating around me. The waitresses circulate with platters of finger food. I can't eat a thing so I shake my head politely.

From across the room I catch Guy's glance and smile back. A look of relief crosses his face. Someone comes up to whisper something in Lana's ear. She excuses herself and follows the woman. My sister turns to me and beams. I can see that she is pleased with me.

I smile back mistily. I am more than a little tipsy.

"You're doing very well," she whispers, bestowing me with a truly radiant smile. "I'm *so* proud of you."

Another woman comes to join us. Lena introduces us. I smile and nod politely, then tune out of their conversation. I turn my gaze to the

window. There is a thick layer of snow on the ground and the Barrington's garden looks like a winter wonderland.

From my vantage point I can see the edge of what looks like a massive conservatory. It is softly lit with round yellow lamps and seems to have a mature orange tree in it! The tree is at least seven or eight feet tall with a thick trunk and branches groaning with fruit. Instantly, I am seized by the need to go and have a closer look.

"I'm just going to find the toilet," I tell Lena. I don't want to drag her with me or ruin her party. I just want to look at the tree.

"I'll come with you," she says immediately.

I touch her hand in a stopping gesture. "No, I'll be fine."

She stares at me. "Are you sure?"

"Absolutely."

"Okay I'll be right here waiting for you."

I nod and leave the room. The alcohol makes me feel as if I am floating. I drift down the thankfully empty hallway towards the conservatory. I open the door and gasp.

It is not a conservatory at all, but a breathtakingly beautiful orangery. Whoever the Barrington's gardener is, he is a genius of color and texture. He has created a magical garden where everything is in season. Oranges, lemons, limes, bananas, strawberries, chilies. Even the flowering plants are all in bloom.

There are roses, lilies, japonica berries, scarlet willow, and a whole load of other flowers I don't recognize. The rich smell of the earth mixes with the sweet scent of jasmine and fills my nostrils. I move deeper into the garden, my high heels sinking into the soil. Impulsively, I take my shoes off and let my feet feel the cold soil.

Baby steps.

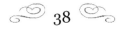

I let my fingers trail over the velvety petals of a white trumpet flower and smile to myself. For the first time since we left the castle I feel glad that I came out. I feel brave and oddly happy.

As I stand there congratulating myself, the door at the opposite end of the entrance I came in from is suddenly opened. I whirl around in a panic and almost laugh with relief. An adorable little boy in blue pajamas and bare feet comes in and closes the door behind him.

For an instant he looks almost ghostly pale standing against the dark of the night. Then he takes another couple of steps closer and comes into the circle of light cast by one of the lamps. I know instantly that he must be Lana and Blake's son, Sorab. He has his mother's beautiful eyes, the lashes long and sweeping down his cheeks, but the rest of his face is all his father's. Lena was right, he is indeed adorable.

"Hello,' I say, pleased by his appearance. I thought we had arrived too late and I had missed the opportunity of meeting him or his sister.

"Hello," he replies, staring up at me with huge eyes.

"What are you doing up at this time of the night?"

"I had a bad dream and I couldn't sleep. I was looking out of my window.' He turns and points to a first floor window across the garden. Next to it is a balcony with a wrought iron spiral staircase coming down from it. "And I saw you here. I thought you were a Christmas angel."

I laugh, all the stress and dread of tonight momentarily gone. "A Christmas angel? That is certainly not me."

"Why are you here on your own then?" he demands.

"I was at your parents' party, but I came in here to look at the orange tree."

He rubs his eyes and yawns. "Oh."

"So you had a bad dream, huh?"

"Yeah," he confirms, nodding solemnly.

"Want to come over here and tell me what it was about?" I ask, pointing to a bench behind me.

He walks over and we sit next to each other. His feet do not touch the ground and there is about a foot between us. He looks up at me and I raise my eyebrows encouragingly.

He slouches. "I dreamed of a dragon."

"You did?" I can't help exclaiming.

He looks at me with curious, surprised eyes. "Don't you dream of dragons then?"

I shake my head. "Never." I smile. "Is it very exciting to see a dragon in your dreams?"

He swings his legs back and forth. "Sometimes. I like it best when I'm flying with them though."

Completely entranced, I turn more fully in his direction. "What were you doing with them this time?"

"I was fighting an evil, fire-breathing dragon. I won, but my horse died in the fire." His voice sounds sad.

"Oh my. That's awful," I say, shocked by the violence in such a small child's nightmare.

"What are you doing out of bed, Sorab?" a man's voice rings out.

I nearly jump out of my skin. I swivel my head around and see a tall, broad man standing at the doorway. My breath catches. He is without doubt the most beautiful man I have seen in my whole life. Not even in magazines have I seen a face such as his.

Thick, straight charcoal hair falls onto his forehead. His eyebrows are straight and strong and his cheekbones and jaw are sculptured ivory. He is not wearing a suit like all the other men, but a black shirt rolled up at the sleeves. There are tattoos curling out of them. It is immediately obvious that he is different than all the other men at the party.

Like me he doesn't belong here.

My heart is still pounding from being startled by him, and my whole body is urging me to run back to my sister's side, but something else, something I've never felt before roots me to the spot. As still as a statue I gape at him.

Five

Sofia

"Uncle Jack," the boy shouts delightedly and, jumping to the ground, runs to him.

The man grins and lifts him up easily, and swings him around. I am filled with a strange sense of loss. I am the outsider. I am always the outsider.

I stand nervously. I wish they were not blocking the doorway so I could slip out unnoticed and return to my safe spot between Lena and the Christmas tree. I even contemplate going out through the door the boy had come in from, but have to discard that idea quickly since I have no idea how to get back to the main room from the garden.

"I should be getting back to the party," I squeak.

The man puts the boy down and looks at me. His eyes are so blue they burn like twin Bunsen burner flames in his face. My pulse begin to race.

"What's the rush, Sofia?" he asks.

I freeze with horror and stare at him in astonishment and shock.

Oh good God! No. He knows me.

It cannot be.

Surely even I can't be that unlucky.

This is my first trip out since my rescue. How is it possible that I've run into someone who has been inside me before? Still, how could I have not remembered such a beautiful man? Impossible even in my drug fueled haze. Maybe he recognized me from those videos that Valdislav made. *Open your legs, Sofia. Wider, Sophia. Wider still, Sofia.* Burning shame rushes up my neck and face.

He narrows his eyes. "Are you okay?"

"How do you know me?" I gasp.

He shrugs. "Someone mentioned that Lena was bringing her sister. Since I know all the other guests I guessed you had to be her."

The relief that pours into my body is indescribable. My knees feel weak with it. *He doesn't know me. He doesn't know me.*

He holds his hand out. 'Jack Irish."

I hesitate, looking down at his large, strong hand for a few seconds, then, *It's all right Sofia. It's safe.* I place mine in his. An electric current zaps me at the point of contact and goes right through me, making me jump. I snatch my hand back.

His eyes glitter with curiosity.

I know I am behaving strangely, but I cannot help myself. I feel vulnerable and exposed as if those blue eyes can see into my very soul. Fortunately, at that moment I see Lana and my sister coming towards us.

"There you are," my sister calls gaily, but she can't keep the tinge of worry out of her voice.

"Hello, Jack. I see you've all met." Lana looks down at her son. "What do you think you're doing out of bed, young man?"

"Look, Mummy, you're standing under the mistletoe,' Sorab cries gleefully pointing up.

We all look upwards, and not only Lana, but even Lena and I are standing under a garland of mistletoe, red apples, and rosettes of colored paper suspended from the ceiling.

For a few seconds a strange tension fills the air. The air throbs with it. I shift my eyes to Lana. There is a strange strained smile on her face. Before I can figure out what is happening Jack curls his powerful hands around my upper-arms and, bending his head, brushes his cool, beautifully full lips against mine.

I am so stunned I stop breathing. As he lifts his head, I stare up at him with disbelief. His eyes are dark, his jaw is clenched, and there is a muscle jerking furiously in his cheek.

"Merry Christmas, Sofia," he mutters.

I blink in confusion, my whole body in an incredible turmoil. He kissed me. A total stranger just kissed me. Why did he pick me? Do I look sluttish? Did I act skanky or cheap?

Valdislav used to say I always acted like I 'wanted some' but I thought he was lying. He said I was a natural born whore. Women like me were meant to be hookers. All kinds of images suddenly whirl into my head.

Men doing things to me. Touching me. Entering me. Forcing me. Me smiling, smiling, smiling. Always pretending to be the happy hooker. Giving everybody their money's worth.

The memories come faster and faster. I don't know what to do to stop these ugly images. I open my mouth, but no sound will come out. I forget my

surroundings and feel myself sway. I am going to faint.

In a flash Lena pushes forward and takes both my hands in hers. I fight to focus my gaze on her. Her lips are smiling, but her eyes are blazing fiercely, willing me not to fall apart.

"It's okay," she whispers passionately in Russian. "I'm here. Nothing can happen to you while Guy and I are around. You know that. He was just being friendly. It is their custom. It means nothing."

I close my mouth and nod. She is right. Of course, she is right. The images are already whirling away. I'm safe. Nothing bad has happened. I simply over-reacted. It was the shock of having a man's lips on mine. I did not expect it. I clench my hands into fists to stop them from shaking.

I know everyone is staring at me with shock. What a fool I have made of myself. I dare not even look up and meet

Jack's gaze. He must think I am weird or crazy.

"Let's go get a drink, I know I could do with one," Lena says gently.

I smile shakily and nod.

"You guys go ahead while I put this little monster back in his bed," Lana says.

"Nah. I've got him. I'll catch you guys later," Jack says.

I still don't look at him.

"Nite, nite, Sorab," Lena says.

As for me, I am unable to utter a single sound.

"Come on, Sofia." My sister puts her hand on my arm and starts to guide me away.

As we leave the corridor I turn my head towards the glass walls and see Jack with Sorab sitting on his shoulders moving quickly through the snow covered garden.

Sorab is gripping his head and laughing at something he said. My gaze lingers on them for a while longer as

 50

they start to climb the wrought iron
staircase before I turn resolutely away.

How strange.

My heart is calling to him.

Six

Jack

I read to Sorab and stay with him until his eyelids flutter closed. It is only then that I no longer see Lana in his little face.

For so long I loved her.

For so long I thought she was mine.

I'd spent my whole life protecting her, caring for her, wanting her, then one day, without any warning, she belonged to someone else, and there was not a fucking thing I could do about it.

I was young. I thought I had time.

Fool, that I was, I was waiting for the right moment. I was so sure I knew her. I thought there would not be a single thing she could do that would surprise me. How fucking wrong I was.

Right under my nose, she went and sold herself to a billionaire banker to pay

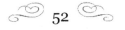

for her mother's cancer treatment. What could I say? I was a student. I didn't have a pot to piss in. She needed the money. He wanted a mistress. It was an arrangement made in hell.

The rest, as they say, is history.

I was furious with myself for being so cocksure, but I hated Blake so much I wanted to kill him. Day and night I couldn't think of anything else but him touching her, making love to what I had marked as mine. It drove me fucking crazy so I left the country. I joined Doctors Without Borders and asked to be sent to Africa.

Losing Lana broke my heart, but Africa destroyed and scarred me forever. There, I lost my faith in humanity. The poverty, the cruelty, the corruption, the suffering, the massacres, the injustices, the daily indignities I witnessed.

Even now there are nights I can't sleep for the terrible things I have seen. The corpses rotting in the heat, the women mad with grief, and the staring,

starving children. Their dark eyes haunt me still.

At that time my life was meaningless to me so I would specifically request to go to the most dangerous war-torn areas. Unprotected by UN trucks, I went into rebel controlled areas to rescue children from orphanages. The 'rebels' were usually merciless psychopaths intoxicated with the power that comes from unadulterated brutality, but I had no fear of death.

I stood in front of men wielding machine guns and dared them to shoot me. I think I shocked them. They called me the Mad White Man, but they were intrigued by me. Sometimes they brought their wounded to me and I healed them. My attitude was simple. Bring a broken body to me and I'll never turn it away.

That's what I was put on this earth to do.

I watch Sorab's little chest as it moves, even and deep. Sometimes he will smile in his sleep. Today he doesn't. I love this kid. I think I transferred all the love I had for his mother onto him. When I look at Lana now, that burning love is gone. From its ashes has come this pure love for this tiny human she created. He is my godson and he is my hope. In this ugly world this little gentle soul is sprouting quietly. Maybe, just maybe, one day he will make a difference.

With the back of one finger I gently stroke his silky hair.

"Sleep, little Sorab."

Quietly, I stand and walk to the door. I open it, take one last look at the sleeping child, and shut it quickly so the freezing air doesn't get in. I key in the alarm code and wait for the green light to come on before I turn away.

I stand on the metal platform for a second looking down at the snow covered garden. It's beautiful. A sigh escapes me. I go down the steps and instead of walking back to the party I stand in the shadows and look in through the tall windows.

I see Lana laughing at something someone has said, and I see Blake listen quietly to a blond man, but my eyes are searching. Searching for a girl in a white dress and enormous, brown eyes. So huge they could light up a man's dark soul.

I find her half-hidden amongst the foliage of the Christmas tree.

"Sofia." I test the name on my lips. My breath mists. Her name is like conjuring up a magic spell.

I watch her smile and nod at the things the people around her are saying, but it is clear that she is miles away. I stare at her. Her hair is in a tight bun at the nape of her neck. She is delicate, tentative and nervous. Like a bird, or a newborn fawn. Definitely not my type. I'm a sucker for girls with long legs. The longer the better. Bold girls who take what they want and leave in the morning without too much fuss.

Yet, she fascinates me. Immensely.

I only kissed her because there was no way in hell I was kissing Lana. That way lay old wounds, confusion, and sleepless nights. I will love Lana forever, but like a sister. Those old dreams are all dead now.

Sofia's reaction to such a simple brush of my lips was astounding. The way she stared up at me. White as a sheet. Shocked. Disbelieving. As if I had reached into her body and ripped out her heart. I thought she was going to fucking faint at my feet.

Her sister must have thought the same. She moved in quickly, held onto her trembling hands tightly, and fiercely said something to her in their native tongue.

I've seen that exact same expression that was in Sofia's eyes once before. When I was in Africa, a thirteen-year old girl was brought in while I was on duty.

Her village had been attacked. Everyone in it was dead. She alone had survived, but she had been gang raped and set on fire. When I came to her she was half-lying, half-sitting on the bed. She looked up at me as I approached.

It was a strange look. If you didn't know better you'd think that person was unaffected by what had happened to them. I remember watching her scratch her leg and swat away a fly that was trying to land on her skin as if a third of her body was not raw and her insides had not been ripped to shreds and hanging out between her legs.

I knew as I treated her burns, sewed her up, and bandaged her as best I could that she would never heal from that trauma. She would forever be shattered inside. When her uncle came from another village a week later to carry her away, I stood outside the clinic under the heat of the African sun. I was so angry with the way things were that I wanted to scream at God.

Look at what you have allowed.
Look. Look.

The uncontrollable fury is gone. I have dulled it with alcohol and mindless activities.

I gaze through the window at Sofia and I wonder what happened to her. Whatever it is it has scarred her for life. Something moves inside me. Old grief. It makes my gunshot wound hurt. It's been a long time since I felt that emotion. I rub the scar through my shirt. Somewhere in the distance I hear a fox calling.

Silently, I pray that one day a man will brush his lips against hers and she won't shake with terror, but curl her hands around his neck and kiss him back. I pray she will find the happiness I never did.

The snow swirls around me. It's freezing without my coat.

I should go back in and join the party, but I don't have the heart for it. I can't stand around sipping mulled wine.

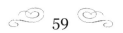 59

Remembering the burnt girl has brought back memories I thought I'd forgotten.

I go through the rose arbor that looks truly glorious in summer and out to the front of the house. Leticia lets me in the front door.

"Get me my coat, will ya?"

She smiles at me flirtatiously. She's tall with long legs, my kind of girl, but I really don't need to fuck Blake's staff. "You're not leaving surely?" she dimples at me.

"Yeah. Merry Christmas to you."

I go down to my local. It is thick with happy people. Christmas carols are playing in the background. Someone calls my name. I turn around. Tommy waves. He is holding a pint glass. Not of beer, but whiskey! I wave back.

I already know how the night will end. I'll get drunk. Maybe someone will be stupid enough to pick a fight with me. Goddamn, I could do with punching someone's face in tonight. Or better still a girl with long, lean legs will offer her bed for the night.

It's Christmas Eve, after all.

Seven

Sofia

https://www.youtube.com/watch?v=d4
QnalIHlVc
(Private Dancer)

The rest of the party passes in a blur.
People come to speak to us and
somehow I smile and nod, and
sometimes I even make little sounds of
polite agreement, but in truth I hear
nothing. My lips are throbbing where his
skin touched mine and my mind replays
that moment incessantly.

The way my heart had jumped and
soared like a bird released after a long
imprisonment. It's just a custom, Lena
said. He could have kissed anyone of us.
He only kissed me because I was the
only single one there. But I saw the odd
expression in his eyes, the tenseness in
his jaw, and the furious tick in his cheek;

I know that there was something more at play.

We say our goodbyes in the foyer. The milk and cookies are still waiting for Santa. I pull the edges of my coat tighter around my body and look up the curving stairs. I wonder if Sorab is off flying with dragons in his dreams. I would have liked to have known him better.

Someone opens the door and a gust of cold wind blows in. Guy turns towards me and I smile and walk towards it. Robert, our chauffeur drops us off outside Guy's offices. We take the elevator to the roof of the building where a helicopter is waiting to take us home.

As we walk towards the helipad, Lena makes a throw away comment about the fact that I have apparently agreed to spend the day after Christmas at a place called Kids Rule. She smiles at me, obviously very pleased about the idea.

"What?" I stare at her alarmed. Someone took those polite noises I made seriously.

Her eyes narrow. "Don't you remember? You told Lana you would."

The alcohol in my stomach churns making me feel quite sick. "I did? I'm sorry, Lena. I honestly can't even remember agreeing to go, but you'll have to tell her that I can't make it to this thing, whatever it is."

My sister squeezes my hand. "Hey, stop panicking. It's just lunch with some underprivileged kids. Besides, it's not like you'll be going on your own. I'll be there too."

Phew. The instinctive fear I feel recedes. If it is going to be just children, then there's no harm. I could go along and simply watch. I like children and enjoy their company. Exhaling with relief, I press my hand to my stomach. "So we'll be having lunch with some kids?"

"Exactly. Most of those kids will not have had a proper Christmas dinner so that will be their great feast with turkey and the whole works thrown in. Lana said they'll even have a Santa coming with presents for everyone."

"I see. That's really nice of Lana."

"Well, it's actually one of the charities set up by Lana. The lunch is being held at Kids Rule in Kilburn."

"Kids Rule?" I ask with a smile.

"It's a club where children from poor or broken homes can go to be safe while they learn or amuse themselves. They hold all kinds of free classes. Dancing, singing, music, drama, self-defense, computer. The idea is to turn them away from drugs and alcohol by engaging them in fun activities that they enjoy."

"How wonderful."

She shrugs. "Who knows? Maybe you'll decide to volunteer your time."

I say nothing. The idea is foreign, but not terrifying.

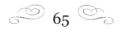

My sister smiles warmly. "No pressure. I'll come with you to start with and if you don't enjoy it we won't go anymore, okay?"

I nod slowly.

Baby steps.

By the time we get home it is late. There is a thick layer of snow and the castle looks enchanted and mythical, like something you'd find in a storybook. Guy and Lena bade me goodnight and enter the west wing while I make for my living quarters in the tower.

I stop outside the door and glance up. Rita has been in earlier to turn down the bed, light the fireplace and switch on the lights. They make the stained glass windows glow like jewels in the dark night. It looks lonely and exposed up here. At night when there are storms I can hear wind howling outside, but I like it. The walls are thick and I feel completely safe.

I close the door behind me, lock it, and take the fifty-seven winding stone stairs up to my living quarters. My palm trails the stone walls and my shoes echo loudly. Sometimes, as I go up these steps, I remember those irresistible fairytales Mama used to read for us. Every Princess who lived in a tower was eventually saved by her Prince.

I am no Princess.

No one is going to come and save me.

Which is fine with me.

I open my door and breathe in the familiar scent of lavender candles. This is my little sanctuary and I *love* it. Everywhere you look there are delicious nooks and corners full of little things that Lena or the staff have given me. When Guy knew I wanted to live in this tower he had it decorated so that the entire suite, which contains a salon, a bedchamber, and a luxurious bathroom, resembled something straight out of a Medieval movie set.

There is a queen size bed draped with a regal green brocade canopy, a writing table, a tall armchair, and a gorgeous parlor sofa hidden behind velvet curtains where I often curl up with a good book. The orange flames flickering in the fireplace make the place look deliciously warm and cozy. I take my shoes off and walk barefoot on the deep pile carpet into the bathroom.

In the bathroom there are Roman mosaic tiles and a sunken bath set in marble under a star-covered ceiling. I go and stand in front of the mirror. For a few seconds I look at myself curiously. There is a flush on my cheeks. It must be the alcohol.

I release the pins in my hair, my one claim to beauty, and it falls in shining, golden-brown waves down to my waist, but today my attention is arrested by my eyes. They seem different. They glitter.

I touch my lips. A man kissed me tonight and I didn't feel revolted. In fact, I wanted him. For the first time in my life I *wanted* a man.

I close my eyes and I see his face. The hot blue eyes, the hard cheekbones, the straight, dark hair falling over his forehead. Something curls in my stomach. I think of the tattoos snaking out of his rolled up sleeves and feel an ache between my legs. I want to touch those tattoos and follow the ink. Let it lead me wherever ...

I take a deep breath. In the mirror I'm scowling.

Have you ever seen a movie director shooting a green screen scene? It's weird. You can't feel anything since the actor does his part against a green screen with no references to real life. Later in dark booths, engineers and technicians will add sounds, backgrounds, smoke, bleeding people. Whatever makes the scene believable.

Well, a green screen movie take is what my life resembles.

I go about my life in front of a green screen. There is no background, no sounds or references to make sense of the scene. It's quite weird, but generally it serves its purpose.

However, on a night like this, when my heart has allowed the green screen to fool it into forgetting what it shouldn't have and yearns instead for what it can never have, I will allow myself to add background to my movie. This is the only way to remind myself. This is reality. This will cure me from wanting beautiful men I can never have. Men like Jack Irish.

I open my eyes, unzip my dress and let it fall to the ground. My skin is smooth, my breasts are smallish and perky, and my waist trim. I am wearing white cotton panties.

I take them off.

My hips are gently curving and my legs are shapely from all the hard work I

did as a child. There are a few silver scars on the insides of my thighs, but they cannot be seen when I stand like this. You have to spread my legs to see them.

Very slowly, with my heart hammering in my chest, I turn around and stand with my back to the mirror. Then I do what I have not done ever since I came to this gorgeous castle. Taking a deep breath, I bring the thick curtain of my hair over one shoulder, and swivel my head to look at my back. My hands clench involuntarily.

There it is.

My life with the green screen removed. Replaced with the background of a dirty brothel. As if it happened yesterday I feel again the cut of the rough ropes around my wrists and ankles, hear the taunts and laughter of the men, smell the acrid scent of burning flesh, and hear my own screams of horror and excruciating pain.

There it is for all to see.

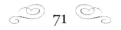

Across my back is the poignant reminder of my real worth.

Branded like common livestock with crude fire-heated irons are the marks of my ownership. The letters are blotched since I flailed too much, but you can still clearly make the words out.

Valdislav Mikhailov

Eight

Jack

I wake up to the sound of thunder and rain hitting the windows. Great. It's fucking raining on Christmas Day and there's a banging in my skull. Fuck. I'm too old for this.

I was all right while we were playing that comfortingly juvenile game Fuzzy Duck, but when it moved on to Dirty Pint and I called the toss wrong three times in a row, I was gone. For fuck's sake, Tommy was drinking Scotch, I was drinking beer, Liam was on the Guinness, and the girls were drinking wine and cocktails. A little bit of all that into a one-pint glass. Even thinking about it now makes me want to puke.

I grab the sides of my head and groan.

"Merry Christmas," a voice next to me says.

I freeze. I don't even remember picking up a woman.

Her head pops up in my vision. Blonde, fake eyelashes, smeared lipstick, but not bad looking. I kind of vaguely remember her. Top heavy, pink top, leather miniskirt. She was so tanked up she had to take a piss behind some bushes in someone's garden. Fuck, I wasn't much better. We staggered up her stairs and fell through her door.

"You're a sight for sore eyes, Jack Irish," she says.

Her voice goes right through me. I scowl and lift up my hand in the universal gesture of STOP TALKING! The gesture is lost on her.

"What's not to like? You're breathing, aint ya?" she says, and laughs raucously. It is like machine gun fire in my head.

"Fuck," I mutter. I got me a talker.

Her hand reaches for my crotch. I grab her wrist and look at her with cold eyes. "Don't."

She frowns. "That's not what you said last night."

"Yeah, well. Morning's always a bitch." I jack-knife upright, my feet landing with a thud on her wooden floor. A cold, full condom squelches under my foot, and pain explodes in my head.

"You're different today," she accuses sulkily.

Squinting, I pull my underpants on and grab my shirt off the floor. Shrugging into it I glance at her as I do the buttons. "I'm sorry. My head's pounding and I'm really not in the mood to engage in chit chat."

She breaks into a cajoling tone. "Do you want me to make you breakfast or something?"

I practically gallop into my jeans. "I appreciate the offer, er ..."

"Melanie," she supplies.

"It's really sweet of you, Melanie, but I'm kind of in a hurry." Sitting on the bed I pull on my socks.

She touches my arm. "We had fun last night didn't we? We were good together, weren't we?"

I suppress the bile rising up my throat. I hate clingy women. Women who can't take a hint. You need to hit them over the head with a fucking brick to make them understand. "Yeah, sure."

"Maybe, we can meet up for a drink some time, huh?"

I smile tightly. "You know, sweetheart, maybe not."

"Why do you have to be so horrible? It's Christmas morning."

I pull my arm through one sleeve and I open the door to her studio apartment. "Merry Christmas," I say as I make my exit.

The elevator doesn't work so I take the stairs. It smells of stale urine. Outside it is pissing down with rain. All the magical snow is gone. I look at my watch. It's already ten thirty.

I open the door and step out into freezing cold rain. It lashes down on me, soaking through my clothes very quickly. The shops are all closed and the streets are deserted. Water runs down the pavement in rivulets. My boots squelch with rain water as I walk down the road. I get to Kilburn High Street and decide not to bother going back to my apartment. My mother's house is less than fifteen minutes away. I set off for it. I'm outside her door in ten. Her neighbor is peeking out of her window. When she catches my eyes she gives a little wave.

I nod and put my key into my mother's door. As soon as the door opens I am surrounded by the smells of a massive Christmas dinner cooking.

She comes out of the kitchen wearing her apron over her new red dress. It has lace on the collar and pearl buttons. Her cheeks are rosy with the

heat from the kitchen, and her watery-blue eyes widen with surprise at the sight of me.

It makes me feel guilty. This day is important to her. I shouldn't have rolled out of some bird's bed and turned up here like a drowned rat. I should have got a taxi home, freshened up, and arrived with her present.

"Merry Christmas, Ma."

"You'll catch your death of cold. Go on. Git." She shakes her head and scolds as she shoos me towards the bathroom.

I hurriedly peel off my sodden clothes and get into the shower. Standing under the hot cascade I feel the life slowly come back into my frozen limbs. Ten minutes later I get out.

My mother has left a clean towel and clothes for me on a chair. I towel myself dry and swipe the steam off the mirror with my palm. A stranger's face stares back. His eyes look frighteningly empty. Just pieces of blue glass stuck into the sockets. I'm worth millions, my name is well known, and my expertise is greatly sought after, but none of it gives me any happiness.

I make my hand into the shape of a gun, point it at my reflection and 'bang.' "You died in Africa, Irish," a nasty voice in my head says.

"Not too shabby for a zombie, then," I say to the voice and turn away.

I get dressed and go into the kitchen.

Ma is sitting at the table peeling potatoes. Through the glass door of the oven I can see a large turkey roasting.

She glances up at me. "You drink too much. You look terrible."

I open the fridge and take a beer out. I open the cap, flip the bottle opener back into the drawer, and sit at the kitchen table.

"You'll kill yourself at this rate," she sniffs.

"Leave it out, Ma," I mutter. I'm fucking thirty. I don't need this shit. I take a long drag of the cold beer while my mother glares at me.

"So I'm just supposed to stand back and watch you kill yourself, am I?" she demands.

"Oh for God's sake. It's fucking Christmas, Ma."

She sniffs again. This time more dramatically. "Ever since you came back from Africa you've never been the same. What happened to you there? Why can't you talk about it and get it off your chest?"

"Nothing, Ma. Nothing happened. Do we have to talk about that now? Today? When I feel like shit?"

I glare at her and deliberately take another long drag. She takes a deep breath. I can see the thoughts running through her head. She doesn't want to spoil the day.

"I've made the pies for your Christmas lunch with the kids tomorrow," she says finally.

I put the bottle on the table. It has already had the desired effect. My head has miraculously cleared. Nothing like the hair of the dog. I smile at my mother. She went to all this trouble. I'll make the effort. "Thanks, Ma."

She smiles back. "That's all right, Jack. I'm just glad you've come around for Christmas. I miss you, you know."

I don't tell her I miss her too. Because I don't. I never miss anyone. The days when I wanted people are gone. Now people are like the tide. They come, they go. While they are in front of me I'll give them my time, but I want nothing from them. Nothing. Not things. Not money. Not power. Not love. Nothing.

Outside my head my mother carries on talking. She tells me about the café down the road closing down, the kids stealing her doorbell, her nosy neighbor. I hear snatches.

"I told him to get lost."

"Asking me if you've found a girl yet. What a bloody cheek ..."

I turn to glance out of the window. It's still raining hard. For some weird reason I think of the girl in the orangery.

Sofia Seagull.

Not because I want her or anything like that. Just because she is different. Different from all the other women I have known.

Nine

Sofia

"**O**pen your presents then," Lena orders.

She is still in her nightgown and fluffy dressing gown. Her hands are clasped in front of her chest and she is so excited she can barely sit still. I look at her and smile. My heart fills with love for her. She is like a big child. Full of light and enthusiasm. Outside, the rain is slicking down on the windows. Inside my tower suite, it is warm and faintly scented with the smell of coffee.

"Let's open our presents together," I say, looking at the pile of packages on the bed. There are three, one each from her and Guy for me, and one from me to her.

"No, no, you go first," she urges. "I want to see your face when you see our presents."

"Okay," I say, and just to see her reaction, I slowly take a sip from the steaming mug of coffee she brought for me.

"Oh for God's sake,' she screeches.

I laugh at the expression on her face.

She snatches a flat package and thrusts it into my hand. "Open this one first. It's from me."

Putting my mug down on my bedside table and crossing my legs, I take it from her. With a smile I shake it. It rattles.

"Coupons or tickets?" I guess.

"Just open it," she cries impatiently.

I tear open the wrapping and lift the lid of the cardboard box. I take out the folded letter inside and read it.

"Oh," I exclaim. "You got me driving lessons." Immediately my heart starts thudding with fear. I can't get into a car alone with a man and be in such close proximity with him for an hour at a time. I look up at her trying to smile. Not wanting to burst her bubble of excitement.

She grins at me. "The instructor is a woman."

I exhale through my mouth. "Oh, thank you. What a wonderful present, Lena. I'd love to be able to drive into the village myself and not trouble someone else all the time. Thank you my darling." I lean forward and kiss her.

"The next one. The next one," she squeals excitedly. "This one's from Guy." She pulls away from me and holds out the long oblong box, the kind you use to send posters. It is light, and feels hollow. When I shake it there is no sound.

"Go on then," she urges.

I tear it open and pull out a rolled up piece of paper. I look at her and raise my eyebrows as I unroll it. She just grins widely at me. I run my eyes down the thick paper. For a moment I can't believe my eyes.

"Well?" Lena prompts.

I blink and look up at her in disbelief. "Guy bought me a house in London?"

She nods vigorously. "Yes. You're now the proud owner of your own house."

I stare at her aghast. I don't want to move out of the castle. I love my tower suite. It is the first place I have felt safe. I stupidly thought I would be able to live here forever.

"What's the matter?" Lena asks.

"You don't want me to live here anymore?" I gasp.

Her face crumples. "What? No. No, of course not. This house is not for you to live in. It is for you to rent out and earn your own money. This way you will be financially independent."

The backs of my eyes burn. "Oh. I don't know the first thing about owning a house in England or renting it out."

"Guy's secretary will find a tenant and arrange everything for you. You don't have to do a thing. You can learn at your own pace, okay?"

My eyes fill with tears. I try to blink them away, and Lena leans in and hugs me tightly.

"You are my heart, Sofia. My heart. One day you will find a wonderful man and you will leave this castle to go to him. It will sadden me greatly, but I will be happy for you. However," she grins wickedly, "until that day you're all mine. This is your home, silly."

We clutch each other and cry.

I dash away my tears with the backs of my eyes. "I feel terrible. Your gifts are so wonderful, and I've only got you a little thing from the village shop."

"Oh, Sofia. I will love whatever you give me with all my heart. If you've got it for me, it will be perfect."

Suddenly there is an odd noise outside the door. It sounds like a muffled shriek.

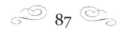

"What the hell is that?" I ask.

She grins. "That's your present from Irina." She gets off the bed. "Don't move," she warns and goes out to open the door.

I hear whispering and then ...

Oh my God!

A golden retriever puppy makes a mad dash into my room! I clasp my hands over my cheeks with shock. My very own dog! I stare at the little thing with unconcealed delight. Lena, carrying Irina, and the nurse come into my room, and all of them are looking at me. I can't say a word.

"She's already toilet trained, but she doesn't have a name yet," Lena says.

Irina struggles in her mother's arms. She wants to get down and play with the puppy, but Lena says, "Wait until Aunty Sofia has met her first." She looks at me. "Go on then. She was found abandoned in a sack by the roadside. Left to die because she has a little limp.

One of her legs is shorter than the others."

"What?" I whisper aghast.

"So she's going to need a lot of love and attention."

I turn away from my sister and look at the little mad thing. Indeed, the pup does have an odd gait, but it is actually quite adorable. How could anyone do that to such an innocent little thing?

"I'll love her to my dying day," I tell Lena staring at the dog.

My mind races ahead. I imagine teaching her all kinds of things. She can sleep on my bed. I'll take her with me when I go for my dawn walks. Oh my God. The fun we'll have together. I get off the bed and fall to my knees. The ball of fur comes up to me and cautiously sniffs my knee, and that is the moment I burst into sobs of pure happiness.

I swear I've never felt so happy in all my life.

Ten

Sofia

We arrive in London with time to spare. Guy comes down in the elevator with us, kisses Lena and helps us into the waiting car. He closes the door and stands on the sidewalk watching as Robert, his London chauffeur, drives us away. Both of us turn back to watch him and I can't help the strange sadness that comes into my heart that I don't have a man to wave me goodbye and love me the way Guy loves my sister.

Edgware Road, full of middle-eastern shops and restaurants, morphs higher up the road into Kilburn High Street. I have never been to these areas so I gaze out of the window curiously. By the time we turn off the busy high street and into the estate with the high rise apartments, I can immediately see the poverty of the area.

As it happens we arrive at the parking lot of Kids Rule at the same time as Lana. She gets out of a cute white Geely Panda and waves to us.

"Isn't her husband a billionaire?" I ask my sister.

"Lana doesn't like to display her wealth when she comes here. She says, 'why rub it in their noses'."

"Hey," Lana calls coming over to us. She is dressed simply in a turtleneck red jumper, faded blue jeans, brown boots and a short leather coat. Her long hair is tied up in a ponytail and her face is scrubbed of make-up, but she is still very beautiful. "So glad you could make it."

We kiss each other's cheeks and head towards the wooden entrance of the one-story building. Inside, there are other people already there. They smile at us and call out greetings.

Lana walks down a corridor with us and explains the uses for the rooms on either side of us. Some with desks and chairs are for helping children with their studies, others, with musical instruments, mirrors, sports equipment, or rubber mats, are dance studios, gyms, and music rooms.

At the end of the corridor we come to a set of doors and enter what Lana calls the main hall. It is hung with Christmas decorations and is already half-full of children. They are milling about in small groups talking loudly and laughing.

"Here is where everybody comes to have fun. We hold dances, competitions and concerts here," she explains.

The kids immediately surround us. They are a bold lot. Throwing questions to Lana about Lena and me. Lana introduces us and I follow my sister's example and give a small wave when my name is mentioned.

From the corner of my eyes I see a thin girl with curly brown hair sitting alone on the bench. She is leaning her back against the wall behind her and has her knees pulled up. There is an open book resting on her thighs and she is coloring or drawing something into it. The reason she catches my eyes is because of the way she seems utterly oblivious to all the noise and activity around her.

For a while Lena and I answer the children's curious questions.

"Where are you from?"

"Where's Russia?"

"Have you seen a bear before?"

"Are you're going to be our new teachers?"

My eyes keep flicking back to the girl on the bench. Not once has she raised her head or showed any interest in us.

Eventually, I excuse myself and walk towards her. She can't be more than eight or nine years old. I don't

know why, but I feel almost connected to her. I sit down next to her on the bench. She doesn't turn to look at me. Her eyes are hidden by the curls that hang over her cheeks. I glance at her book. She's drawing a scene with a castle, a girl in a long dress and a man on a horse.

"That's a nice drawing," I say.

Silently she carries on drawing rows of neat little Vs to denote grass.

"My name is Sofia. What's yours?"

Her little hand is a tight fist around the pen as she gives her drawing her total concentration.

I bite my lip. Somehow I have to get through to her. I can't give up. There's something so sad about her.

"I love horses," I say quietly.

She ignores me.

"You should draw a tower for your castle."

Her fist falters for a second, but she does not stop or look at me.

"It's the best bit of a castle."

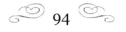

I hear her take a deep breath.

"I know because I live in a castle."

Her pen stops scratching on the paper.

I hold my breath.

She turns her face in my direction, her curls bouncing against her cheeks and her gray eyes huge with curiosity. Instantly, my heart goes out to her. She is a pitiful thing.

"You live in a castle?" she whispers.

I nod. "Uh … huh. I live at the top of the tower."

Her eyes widen to impossible proportions. "You do?"

I nod again. "You have to go up a winding stone staircase to get to my rooms."

Her eyes shine with awe.

"Here. Let me show you." I take my mobile phone out and scroll through my photos. Luckily I took a lot of pictures of my new puppy. I show them to her and she leans in to look at the pictures.

"Is that your puppy?"

"Yes. Her name is Mika."

"She's cute."

I grin. "She's my Christmas present."

A flash of pain crosses her small face. Perhaps she's lost a pet.

I quickly scroll backwards and find a few photographs of the castle taken from the outside. She leans in even closer and gazes at my photos intently.

"Maybe you can come to visit me one day," I say, and suddenly she seems to shrivel up. She jumps to her feet and, gathering her book, runs from the hall.

I stand up, but I can't bring myself to call her back. What would I say? I don't even know her name. Feeling crushed I stare at her small figure rushing away. Damn. I screwed up by being too eager. Who invites a child to their home after a few minutes of knowing them? She probably thought I was some pervert. How stupid I've been.

"How the hell did you do that?"

I swing towards the voice and my cheeks flare up with embarrassment. Oh God! Of all the people in the world why did it have to be Jack Irish who had to witness my failure to connect with even a small child?

Eleven

Jack

"**I**'m so sorry. I didn't mean to make her run away," Sofia apologizes. Her eyes are filled with distress and she looks as if she is about to burst into tears. I stare at her in surprise. Could such innocence still exist?

"Lori hasn't spoken a word to anyone since she has been coming here, which is about six months. You've just had a conversation with her so I don't think you need to be sorry about anything. What you accomplished is close to miraculous."

Her eyes open wide. "Oh!" she exclaims, a flash of pure joy flirting across her face, and I suddenly see she is even more beautiful than I first realized. Her beauty is not diamond-flashy, but mysterious and intriguing, like a string of pearls glowing in the moonlight.

She chews her bottom lip and my eyes rush to the pretty sight. She blushes furiously. Shit, I'm staring at her as if she's the fucking fine print on my life insurance policy.

"Why doesn't she talk?" she asks shyly.

"No one knows. She lives with her mother in one of the apartments around here. I believe her mother is foreign and doesn't mix with the other women either."

She looks troubled, as if Lori really matters to her. "And she has no friends?"

"She doesn't want friends. The other kids have tried to talk to her but she won't even make eye contact. How did you get her to talk to you?"

"She was drawing a castle and I told her I lived in one."

My eyebrows fly upwards. "For real?"

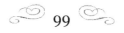

She nods. "Yes, it's in Cheshire. It belongs to my sister and her husband."

I can't help smiling. I've never met anyone who lived in a castle, but she looks like she should be living in a castle. The innocent princess in need of rescue.

"Do you think she'll come back?" she asks worriedly.

"Probably. I think she likes to be around people, but she was not ready to interact. You did really well to make her take that first step."

"But I ruined it. I rushed it and made her run away."

"No, you haven't ruined anything. She's curious about you so she'll be back."

"You really think so?"

"Yeah, I do. You're a natural with a good touch. Why don't you volunteer here, help out with the kids sometime?"

I feel her shrinking away from my suggestion. A frown mars her forehead. "Oh! I don't think that would be possible. It's much too far to come down on a regular basis."

"What wouldn't be possible?" her sister asks, popping up next to us. Her smile and question are casual, but her eyes are watchful and intense. She reminds me of mother tiger, protecting her cubs.

"Nothing really," Sofia mumbles.

Her sister looks at me questioningly and I realize that she could be an ally.

"I was just telling Sofia that she should volunteer to work with the kids since she is such a natural at it, and she was explaining to me that she lives too far away to commute."

Her sister glances from me to Sofia and back to me before breaking into a grin. "Actually, that is an absolutely brilliant idea. We could both come. Let's say once a week. We have an apartment in London so when my husband has business in the city we could even stay overnight."

I look at Sofia and raise my eyebrows encouragingly. "Well. Do you want to see Lori again?"

She clasps her hands and looks suddenly anxious. "But how would we help?"

"Well, you could either teach the children something useful or expand their horizons in some way. Kids Rule is all about empowering these children and turning them away from drugs, gangs and alcohol. You'll have to check with Lana, or one of the girls in the office, but I'm sure you'll be able to work out something between the two of you."

Sofia frowns uncertainly, but her sister is very enthusiastic. "I could give piano lessons, or teach them all the fashion tips I learned while modelling, and Sofia could hold singing classes. She was always the best singer in our family."

"Cool," I say.

Sofia turns to me eagerly. There is a kind suppressed excitement in her face,

as if she doesn't want to get too excited in case she is disappointed. "You really think it's a good idea?"

I grin. I don't know why but the thought of Sofia coming here to teach makes my whole body tingle with anticipation. "Absolutely. As far as I know no one is giving them piano or singing lessons at the moment. And as for the idea of fashion tips from an ex world famous model, you'll have the entire population of girls signing up for your class."

"Thanks, Jack. We'll talk to Lana about this," Lena says.

"No problem," I say.

"I had no idea until Lana told me today that you are *the* Jack Irish," Lena says.

I shrug, vaguely embarrassed. She's making it sound like I'm famous or something.

She smiles. "I must say your name used to come up a lot while I was in the modeling world."

Sofia looks at her sister curiously. "Why?"

She gives Sofia a sidelong glance. "Jack is one of Britain's top plastic surgeons. He runs a very famous clinic in Harley street." She pauses, wrinkles her forehead. "I even know a couple of girls who got their noses done by him. You did an amazing job both times, by the way."

"Thank you," I say quietly.

Then the bell rings and it is time for everybody to get down to the canteen for the big lunch. Lana and the other women have decorated the place with a huge Christmas tree and plenty of tinsel, and there are a lot of gasps and comments of "wicked man" and "cool" from the kids.

Twelve

Sophie

The lunch is fun and the kids appear to thoroughly enjoy themselves. The adults are served wine. I have a glass and it goes straight to my head.

A few times when I look up I catch Jack looking at me, but I become red and get so flustered I have to look away quickly and pretend I did not see him, even though we looked directly at each other. It's so stupid, but Jack Irish has a crazy effect on me.

Later when Santa is giving out gifts there is a loud noise outside. A fight has broken out between some drunks returning from a pub nearby. Jack and another man go to check it out and I find myself waiting for his return nervously. How bizarre, but already I can't bear the thought of him getting hurt.

When he comes back in, the sleeve of his jacket is torn. I breathe a sigh of relief. Some part of me desperately wants to go to him, but my feet will not take me there. It is a good thing I didn't because I notice Susan, a member of staff introduced earlier to me, go up to him, take his hand in hers and examine it.

She stands so close to him that I feel a strange sense of resentment rising in my chest as if he belongs to me and she is intruding. I watch her look up at him with doe eyes and say something, but he shakes his head, extricates his hand from her grasp, and walks away.

Once he leaves, the afternoon seems duller and though I try to join in the games, I can't stop thinking of him.

Before we left, Lena arranged with the woman at the front desk for us to

take a class on the coming Thursday. I must admit I spend the next three days worrying myself sick about it. What if no one comes? What if I screw up or worse, freeze? I chewed my nails right down to raw flesh, but it turns out my anxiety was baseless.

Jack was right, droves of giggling girls flock to Lena's Modelling, Fashion and Make-up Tips class. There are more than forty and we have to use the hall instead of one of the classrooms, but Lena shows no signs of nervousness, in fact, she is brilliant.

She starts off by showing them some simple catwalk moves then turns the class into a sort of finishing school lesson. Which I think is really cool. All these little girls from the estate who will have more etiquette than nineteenth century debutantes.

Her class is interesting even to me. She teaches them little tips that models employ. Apparently they don't say cheese or sex when they want their photos to look pouty and sexy. They say prune.

"Try it," she says, and more than forty little girls echo her and laugh at the expressions of those sitting next to them.

To my great surprise halfway through Lori turns up, but she stays at the back of the hall and does not interact with anyone. Once, I catch her giggling to herself at one of Lena's jokes.

An hour later Lena ends the class by telling the girls to bring their make-up bags the next time. As soon as Lena says, "See you next week," Lori jumps up and makes for the door, not however, before she catches my eyes, and flashes me a shy smile.

I grin back, pleased that she made that bit of contact with me.

Most of the girls immediately mill around Lena, so I wave to her and go into the classroom next door to conduct my singing class. My group is very much smaller, seven girls, but they are sweet, eager little things, and I forget to be nervous. Sitting at the piano I completely enjoy the session. At the end of it I feel quite proud of myself.

Baby steps.

I pack up my stuff, get into my coat and walk out to the foyer. As I open the door I see Lena leaning against the reception counter talking to Jack. He has obviously come from work and is dressed in a white shirt and a pair of black trousers. He turns his head to look at me and my heart starts pounding so madly I can barely say hello.

"How did the class go?" he asks.

"It was okay," I reply as casually as I can.

I'm wearing a blue jumper and jeans so not even a clear outline is on show, but his eyes run down my body with interest. When his gaze returns to my face, he smiles and says, "Good. Now who wants to join me for something to eat?"

"Not me," Lena says. "Got a hot date with my husband later," she says with a wink. "Besides, I haven't seen my daughter all afternoon and I like to catch a couple of hours with my baby before she goes to sleep. Why don't you guys go off and get something to eat?"

"No, I'll come with you," I say.

Ignoring me she looks from me to Jack. "You'll drop my sister off at our place when you've finished your meal, won't you?"

"Of course," Jack assures suavely.

"That will be great. Please take care of her because she is very precious to me," she says, and smiles at him.

His eyes slide in my direction. "Yes, I agree. She is very precious."

Thirteen

Sofia

Outside the air is damp. There is a cold wind blowing and I pull the edges of my tweed coat closer together. After we wave my sister out of the car park, Jack turns towards me.

"How hungry are you?"

"Very."

He grins a devastatingly sexy smirk, making my stomach twist. Stop it Sofia. He's not for you and this is not a date. He offered to take both Lena and me out, only Lena didn't want to come.

"What kind of food would you like to have?" he asks.

"McDonalds?"

He pulls a face. "You do realize that I'm a doctor and cannot condone eating stuff that is molecularly closer to plastic than food?"

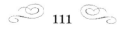

I grin. "I'd still like to try it."

"You've never been to a McDonalds?" he asks incredulously.

"No." I don't tell him that most of my life I was locked up in a brothel. "My sister and her husband always seem to end up in nice restaurants so I've never had the opportunity to try it."

He stares at me oddly.

"What?" I ask defensively.

He shakes his head. "Nothing. I've a better idea though. A friend of mine has a no nonsense burger place. I'll take you there and if after your first bite you don't like it, we'll walk to the McDonalds down the road and order one of their unhappy meals for you."

"Deal," I say with a big smile.

"Come on," he says, lightly laying his hand on the small of my back. He leads me towards a monster of a black Lamborghini.

I laugh. "Are you sure this thing won't bite?"

He holds the door open for me. "The car doesn't bite, I do," he teases, glancing sideways at me.

I feel my face flaming. He's flirting with me. No one has ever flirted with me. Ever. I don't even know what to do. I slip into the car, he closes the door, and goes around the back towards the driver's seat. I look around me curiously. I'm in Jack's car.

The interior is all leather and black trim. The coldness of the leather seat seeps through my jeans and bites into my skin. Once he gets in the air becomes charged with a crackling tension. A whiff of his cologne hits my nostrils. Clean and fresh with a hint of spice, maybe cloves or saffron. I breathe it in and feel my chest tighten. I don't know why he has this effect on me. It is extremely unsettling.

The car roars into life and my eyes slide over to watch his hands. They are large and rough. There are scars on his knuckles. They are not how I imagined the hands of a plastic surgeon would be, but a working man.

I let my eyes slide up his arm and towards his neck, to where his straight black hair lies, as if inviting a woman to rake her hands through it. Before he catches me staring I turn away from the sight. I gaze blindly out of the window. I don't know what is wrong with me. I know I can never have a man like him so I should stop fantasizing about him. It is pointless and I'll just end up getting my heart broken.

It is only a short drive before we arrive at our destination. He parks the car on a single yellow.

"Won't you get a ticket?"

He winks. "Nobody around here would dare give me a ticket."

"Why not?"

"They all come to my free surgery day, and they know I'll ruin their health forever, if they do."

"You'd do that?"

"I don't know. My car is very precious to me," he teases.

We walk to a small burger bar called Earl's Burgers.

Even before Jack has closed the door a gruff voice bellows from the open kitchen, "In the name of Jaysus it's Jackfuckin'Irish." Seconds later a grinning man with close cropped bright red hair and tattoos crawling up his skinny neck vaults over the serving counter and comes over to us. He claps Jack on the back enthusiastically. "Hey dude."

"Alright there, bud," Jack says.

The man's pale blue eyes slide over to me. "And who's this beauty, Junior?"

"Sofia, Paddy. Paddy, Sofia," Jack introduces.

He leans forward and takes my hand in his. His hands are rough and hot. "And how come she's hanging out with the likes of you?"

"She's helping out at Kids Rule," Jack explains shortly.

Paddy's eyes warm up. "Aww … you're a darling, sweetheart."

"Watch it, mate," Jack warns, and there is an underlying ring of steel to his voice that causes even Paddy to jump dramatically.

He raises both hands and takes a long step back.

"Ach, Jack. Don't bite my head off just because your bachelor days are numbered."

I flush to the roots of my hair.

"Jesus, will you leave it?" Jack swears.

Paddy laughs, hits him heartily on the back, and leads us to our table.

"Don't mind him," Jack says tightly. "He drank his IQ down to room temperature."

Unconcerned with the insult, Paddy laughs garrulously. "He wants three babies," he calls out, holding up three fingers while walking backwards. Then, he jumps back over the counter and lands back in the kitchen.

"Well. He's a fun guy," I say casually.

Jack scowls. "God knows what's got into him. He's not usually so … fun."

I grin. "I like him."

He loses the scowl. "Paddy's all right, I guess."

A curvy waitress in a tight pink T-shirt and a pair of pink stretch-jeans comes to our table. She hands me a menu.

"All right Jack?" she says, giving him a bright pink smile.

His lips twitch in greeting. "Hello, Shannon."

I order the Bacon Cheese Big Murphy Burger with chips and a Coke.

"The usual with a side of coleslaw and sweet potato fries," Jack tells the girl.

"Right you are," Shannon says and, taking the menu from me, sashays away.

I pull my eyes away from her departing back, she really does have an amazing figure, and find Jack staring at me. His look is so intense it practically takes my breath away.

"So you're a plastic surgeon," I say nervously.

"Guilty as charged."

"It must be fun playing God with other people's faces and bodies."

He shrugs. "It's just a job."

"Just a job? Don't you like it?"

"Not particularly."

"Really? So why did you become one?"

"It's less hypocritical."

"What do you mean?"

"It's a long story, Sofia."

I lean forward. "I like long stories."

The waitress comes back with two cans of Coke and two glass tumblers.

"Well, I didn't start off wanting to suck fat out of people who are too lazy to get on a treadmill and inject fat into self-obsessed celebrities' faces. When I was young I was an idealist. I wanted to cure the world. I was going to do big things, you know, make a difference."

He stops and frowns.

"Anyway, something happened in my life, and I didn't want to live in England anymore so I joined Doctors Without Borders and they sent me to Africa."

"Oh, wow, Africa!" I interrupt.

For a second he looks bleak. "Yeah, Africa."

"It must have been amazing."

He looks at me expressionlessly. "Africa destroyed me."

"Why?' I ask, shocked.

He drinks his Coke straight from the can. "I realized that there was no way to change the world. Not only is the whole damn system parasitical in nature, it's been deliberately set up to be that way, and little ole me was not going to change it. In fact, my very existence was making the system run. I was actually a cog in a well-oiled machine that was ruthlessly exploiting the poor and the oppressed so that some over-fed capitalist somewhere in the West could make another buck he didn't need."

I gaze at him curiously. "What do you mean?"

He sighs. I can see this is a topic that depresses him. "As a doctor you become the unwitting tool of Big Pharma manufacturers who are busy offloading their out-of-date vaccines and medicines at cut prices. They wanted me to inject poison into those kids."

"Could you not complain to someone?" I ask, aghast.

"The politicians are bought so they turn a blind eye, and the think tanks and government officials stay silent to further their own agendas."

"I can't hardly believe that is going on." What am I saying? Look at the cycle of corruption that kept me enslaved. It was politicians who were my biggest customers.

"It was going on while I was there. It's hard to imagine it is no longer going on. The profits are too big."

"So you left?"

"Not immediately. Even then I thought I could make a difference. I began a campaign of educating the people. In Africa life is cheap. A few bullets. One to the chest and a couple to the stomach. I was very badly wounded and would have died if Blake had not sent in an army to find me and fly me out."

"Oh my God."

"When I came back it was the same shit all over again. Representatives of big pharma constantly in my office pushing the most expensive drugs on me. Basically bribing me with kickback to prescribe those as often as possible. It made me sick and ashamed of the code I had undertaken. Our motto was no longer First Do No Harm, it was Keep Them Sick While You Fill Your Pockets."

He leans back in his chair and I see the scars of his past alive in his eyes.

"Anyway, after that I decided I didn't want to be a doctor anymore. The

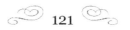

most fitting job for me was to become a plastic surgeon. At least I wouldn't be pretending to be doing something important. I'd simply be tickling someone's neurosis and filling my pockets at the same time."

Fourteen

Jack

"This looks big enough to feed five," she says when her food arrives. I watch the childlike pleasure on her face and suddenly blood is rushing to my ears. *Mine. This one is mine.* The sentiment is barbaric, but it will not be denied and roots itself in my being.

"What?" she asks, her eyes so big and bright, her lush lips parting.

What the fuck? She's like an angel from heaven come to tempt me. As I watch, her tongue comes out, wetting her bottom lip. The air leaves my lungs in a whoosh. Shit. I'm in so much trouble.

"Dig in," I tell her, my voice hoarse.

She takes a bite, her movements self-conscious. Juice runs down the side of her mouth and her tongue comes out to lick it away, and it takes everything I've got not to lean forward and taste her mouth. I'm going to be lying in my cold bed stroking myself to release tonight. She is looking at me innocently.

"Is it good?" I ask with a tight smile. "Or do we need to walk down the road to McDonalds?"

She shakes her head and smiles happily. "No, this is heaven."

"Excellent," I say, and even though I have zero appetite I take a bite out of my burger. "Tell me about you?" I invite.

She swallows and shrugs delicately. "There's not much to tell," she says hesitantly. "I live with my sister, her husband and their daughter."

I nod. "Do you work?"

She shakes her head and the light catches her eyes and they glow like warmed honey with bits of gold pollen. Beautiful. I gaze at her and she blushes.

"What do you do with your time?" I ask. I need to stop behaving like a teenager.

She picks up a chip, dips it restlessly a few times in ketchup, leaves it at the side of her plate, and picks up her glass of Coke. Without drinking from it she puts it back down.

"I know it must seem as if I'd have a whole load of time and be bored all day, but in fact, it's not so. I have my sister, my niece, and my puppy, and the days just fly. Before I know it, it's already bedtime."

I take another bite and try to imagine her life, and just cannot. It seems so different, so alien. Living in the tower of a castle. Spending every day with her sister, a baby, and a puppy.

"Do you guys go out a lot?" I ask curiously.

She laughs nervously. "No, rarely. I'm a homebody, I don't like leaving the castle grounds.' She wipes her mouth and quickly deflects the question back to me. "What about you? Do you go out a lot?"

"Uh, my apartment is basically just a place I go to sleep at night." I don't tell her that half the time I don't even go home to sleep.

"Oh," she murmurs. "How completely different we are. I can't imagine only returning home to sleep. I guess I'm a bit of a loner. I prefer to spend a lot of time on my own."

"Don't you like people?"

"It's not that I don't like people. I find it hard to connect with them. They are not like animals or children, are they? Often they say one thing when they mean another."

"It's very easy to understand people, Sofia. Just bear in mind that 99.99% of the time people are completely motivated by selfish needs. If there is nothing to be gained from their relationship with you they won't be around."

She bites her lip. "So you know that they are around you for personal gain and you don't mind?"

I grin. "I'm around them for personal gain too."

She stares at me. "What do you hope to gain from me?"

Just like that my dick pops into wood. "You? I want you," I say through gritted teeth.

Her cheeks flame. "I ... I can't have a relationship with anybody."

She looks so fearful I feel like I should be protecting her from myself. "Why not?"

Her chin trembles and her long lashes sweep down. "It's a long story."

"I like long stories."

She tries to smile, but it comes out like a grimace. "You won't like this one."

I know she wants me too, but something is holding her back. I reach my hand out to take hers in mine and she jumps as if I have electrocuted her. Looking deep into her eyes I take her hand back into mine and let my thumb stroke it. Her skin is pure silk. She swallows hard.

"I … You'll be disappointed," she stammers.

"Why would I be disappointed?"

"I'm not what you think I am?"

"What do you think I think you are?"

"You think I'm normal. I'm not."

I smile bitterly. "Neither am I."

She shakes her head. "I'm damaged goods." She pauses, her eyes pained. "I'm not … mentally right."

I grip her hand hard. "You'll do fine, just as you are, Sofia."

Her eyes swim with tears and she blinks them away. "You don't understand. I can't be with you, Jack. I can't be with anyone." She stands up suddenly. "I'm sorry, but I have to go."

I stand too. "Let me pay the bill first and I'll take you back."

"No, I'll just take a taxi," she says looking around us nervously. I would lay money on the table that she has never taken a taxi before and she's scared shitless.

"No you fucking won't. I brought you here and I'll take you back."

"Okay, okay," she says, hugging herself. Her face is pale and pinched.

I throw some money on the table and we walk out of the restaurant together while Paddy, the fool, irritatingly shouts, "Three babies. He wants three babies."

We walk in silence towards Lambo and I help her into the car before I get into my seat. She turns towards me. "Thank you for the meal."

I glance at her. Her hands are clutched into little fists on her lap. "You hardly ate anything, but it was a pleasure, nevertheless."

She stares down at her hands in abject misery.

"Hey, relax. It'll be all right," I tell her.

"I'm sorry." The sound is torn out of her throat.

"There's nothing to be sorry for. I'm having you anyway."

Her face jerks up, eyes are glassy, the pupils large. She looks like a scared rabbit, wanting to bolt away. "What did you say?" she gasps.

"What do I look like to you? A fucking quitter. If at first you don't succeed just give up and go away? I'll have you yet, Sofia Seagull," I growl.

"We can't. You can't. I mean, I can't."

"I don't know about you, but I definitely can and will have you."

We lapse into a tight, long silence from the moment I gun the car and join the traffic until we arrive at her home. I turn towards her and she presses her palms to her pale cheeks.

"I really like you, Jack. Can't we just be friends?"

"Friends?" My voice comes out like a sneer. "Yeah sure. We can be friends when you're under me."

Her lips tremble. "Now you're angry with me."

I bite back the frustration clawing inside me and keep my voice even. "I'm not angry with you. I know you want me as much as I do, but you've arbitrarily decided that we shouldn't be lovers. I want you, Sofia. And I'm not taking no for an answer."

"No, you don't understand."

"No, *you* don't understand. There is not one single thing that can stop me from having you. Not you. Not your mental state. Nothing."

She opens her mouth to protest, and at that unsuspecting moment I pull her into my arms and capture her mouth. The second our lips touch is pure magic. Her scent intoxicates me. Drives me wild and makes my soul tremble with need. My tongue pushes out and her mouth opens like a fucking flower. So innocent. No barriers. It's soft and warm inside. I hook her tongue and suck it and moaning she melts against me. The sound makes my cock throb.

With every cell in my body alive I suck her quivering tongue. It's like putting your hand into a socket. The intensity of the desire is a shock to my system. I don't think my heart has beat so fast for a girl since I was a teenager.

My hands reach into her sweater and … suddenly she tears her mouth away. Pressing her back against the door, she stares up at me. She is panting hard and her eyes are bright. Our first kiss and I had to steal it, but stolen stuff is always sweeter. I'm so fuckin' hard I hurt. I pull in a lungful of air, but it is heady with her scent, and it just makes me want to bury my face between her legs.

"Why did you do that?" she gasps.

I drag my fingers through my hair. "Because I wanted to."

"You think you want me, but I'm not what you think I am."

I frown. What kind of cat and mouse game is she playing? "So what are you then?"

"I can't tell you."

"Fucking hell, Sofia. We're not kids here. I'm going to find out one way or another. Just fucking tell me," I growl with a mixture of exasperation and frustration.

She makes a cry like that of a trapped animal in pain. In a flash she hits the door handle and almost falls out of the door. I lunge to catch her, but she dashes into the night.

Breathing hard, I watch her run like the devil himself is after her. She wrenches open the entrance door and disappears into the building. There's a tightness in my chest. I reach forward and pull the passenger door shut. Then my foot slams on the accelerator pad and I speed away.

She'll be mine come hell or high water.

Fifteen

Sofia

You can tell everything from a kiss and Jack Irish's kiss broke me in two. His body told me what his mouth wouldn't. He wants me with the kind of desperation I have never seen in a man. I tasted from the fountain of his need. And his need was vast. Like he wants to lose himself in me. I know I have to stay away from him.

I smile at the guard and walk quickly to the lift. Inside the lift I take deep, calming breaths and try to stop my body from trembling. When I get to the apartment it is silent. The nanny and Irina have still not arrived.

"Is that you, Sofia," Lena shouts from her bathroom.

I clear my throat. "Yeah, it's me," I reply.

"Come and tell me what happened then?"

I go into her bathroom and perch at the corner of her bath. She is leaning her head back and the room is full of fragrant scents. For a few seconds the steam prevents her from seeing my expression. When she does see it she sits up.

"He kissed you," she says in shock.

"Yes," I whisper, touching my swollen mouth.

She looks at me carefully. "Are you all right?"

The question confuses me. "Yes, I think so."

She stands, and with water and soap suds dripping off her beautiful body, she comes to where I am sitting and kneels in front of me. "It's okay to be frightened," she whispers.

My throat closes over so I can't even speak. I just nod as tears begin to run down my face.

Her wet hand reaches out and smears my cheeks. I catch her hand. "I am very frightened." My voice is low and hoarse.

"I know. But I'm here and I'll never let anything bad happen to you."

"He doesn't know about me. About the past."

"Of course not, but you'll take it step by step."

"He wanted us to go out so I told him I was mentally unstable today."

Her head jerks back. "Why on earth did you tell him that? I'm more mentally unstable than you."

"That's not true, Lena. Sometimes I feel as if I'm skating on the very brink of an abyss. One wrong move and I could fall in."

She stares at me, horrified. "That's not true."

"It's true. You and Guy do everything for me. I don't know what I'd be if I had to live alone."

"Well, you will eventually. Step by step. Actually, I was going to suggest that sometimes you can stay here in the apartment alone. I'll go back with Guy, and you can go out with Fiona, or one of the other girls at the center for a drink or a meal in the evening. In the morning you can do some shopping before you come back home." She smiles hopefully. "Would you like that?"

I nod.

"Good. Now, what did Jack say when you told him you're mentally unstable?"

"He said he didn't care."

Her eyes flash with promise. "I like Jack. He's a good guy."

"Yeah, but even good guys don't want a prostitute for a girlfri-."

Lena slaps her hand on my mouth so suddenly it makes my body jerk backwards. She looks at me with fierce eyes. "Don't even let me hear you say that again. What happened to you was not your fault. You were just a child. You didn't choose that life. What happened to you could have just as easily happened to me."

I speak through the hand clamped on my mouth. "But it didn't happen to you. It happened to me." My voice breaks on me.

Lena wraps her arms around me and hugs me tightly. "Oh, Sofia, Sofia. I'm soooo sorry. What I wouldn't do to take your pain away," she cries.

While we are wrapped around each other it occurs to me that I am hurting her. The person I love most in the world. I'm the older sister. It is me who should be taking care of her. I lift my hand and gently stroke her hair. "I have forgotten most of it now,' I lie. 'Soon it will all be gone."

My sister starts sobbing. "You were always an angel. Always. Of all of us you were always the kindest and most gentle."

"Don't cry, Lena. It'll be fine."

She leans away from me and looks into my eyes. "You're still young. You've got to grab life with both hands. The cake, the shoes, the man."

I smile through my tears.

"You have to believe me that your past won't matter a damn to the man who loves you."

I think of the brand on my back and know that it will matter. Valdislav's greatest sexual turn-on was to watch videos of other men fucking me while he rammed into me from the back. He let his eyes alternate between the TV screen and the sight of his name burnt into my back. But what other man is going to want to see Valdislav's mark on his girlfriend's back while he's having sex with her?

"Did you hear what I said?" Lena asks.

"Maybe it's because he's moving too fast." Feeling disloyal to Jack and confused, I cover my face with my hands. "It's not just him. I lose my head when I'm with him too. I think I need more time to process how I am feeling."

"Then take more time. There's no rush. It's not a race."

I nod.

"You take as much time as you want, okay?"

I nod again. No need to trouble her with my worries.

Sixteen

Sofia

The week crawls by at a snail's pace. I fall deeper and deeper in love with my Mika and enjoy watching her grow right before my eyes, but I no longer appreciate my solitude. Every second that I spend alone is full of thoughts of Jack. I replay the kiss a million times in my head. Each time I find myself craving for more.

By the time Thursday comes around I am a total wreck. I put my hair in a French braid and wear my good cream sweater. Lena says it suits me and I have to agree with her. I even wear some mascara and slick on some pink lip gloss.

Lena squeezes my hand. "One step at a time."

We arrive at Kids Rule and Lena goes to her Fashion class, but I don't attend. Instead, I join Lana in the office for carrot cake and tea. I really like Lana. She is kind-hearted.

We sit together eating cake, sipping tea and stapling leaflets that will be handed out in the new branch of Kids Rule in Manchester.

"My sister tells me you grew up on this very Council estate," I say.

Lana gathers two pieces of paper together, staples them, and grins at me. "Yup, but not just me. Jack too."

I raise my eyebrows, surprised and immediately intrigued to find out more about Jack's past. "Really?"

"Yeah. We grew up together." The stapler runs out of staples so she opens a drawer and takes a box out. "My father abandoned my mother when I was very young and Jack kind of took over the job of protecting me, even though he is only a bit older than me."

How lucky she is. First she grows up with Jack protecting her, then she marries a billionaire who worships the ground she walks on. I should have felt envy, but I find that it is impossible to be truly resentful of her. She is so open and warm and kind.

"So you must know him really well," I say softly, my hand playing with a crumb of carrot cake on my plate.

Her forehead furrows as she thinks about my statement. "I don't know, Sofia. I'm not sure anyone really knows Jack. He's very deep. I've known him almost all my life, but I don't think I know the real him."

"What do you mean?"

"For most of my childhood I just knew him as loyal, kind, and protective. He was my rock, but one night he showed a side of him that totally shocked me."

I lean forward curiously. "What was it?"

"My best friend, Billie, me and him had gone to a nightclub and some really rough looking guys wanted to dance with me. I wasn't rude to them or anything, but I refused their offer. They moved away and I thought that was that, but later when we got out of the club, they were waiting for us. They circled us. One of them had a knife. Jack smiled at me and asked me to walk out of the circle and they closed in on him."

The old memory still has the ability to make her shiver.

"That was the first time Jack shocked me. I couldn't recognize him. It was like watching a total stranger. I can still see him now. Shirtless, turning on himself, and snarling like some kind of feral animal, "Come on then. Who's first?"

"I was terrified. You can't imagine how horrible it was. It wasn't like in the movies where the bad guys attack one by one so the hero has a chance to show his fighting skills. They advanced in a group, but Jack was lightning fast. He kicked the one with the knife first. Right in the throat. Before the guy could sink to the ground he had already punched the next one on the nose. Blood sprayed out of him. It happened very fast after that. All I really remember was two more guys dropping like stones. The last one was a coward. He ran away."

"Wow."

"Yeah, he's something else," she murmurs.

"You said that was the first time he surprised you. What was the second time?"

Her eyes become suddenly veiled. Maybe even a little sad. She makes a big production of looking at her watch. "Oh dear. Is that the time? I should be going. I have a hair appointment in less than thirty minutes. Do you mind if we continue another next time?"

"Of course not."

She picks up her tote bag. "Don't bother to do any more leaflets, Sofia. Fiona will finish them later."

"No, it's okay. I don't have anything else to do until my class starts anyway."

She smiles. "All right then. Thanks, Sofia. See you later," she calls as she leaves the room.

While I finish stapling the rest of the leaflets, I speculate obsessively about what the second thing she was referring to might have been. My mind's still on it even as I go to my classroom to prepare for my class. I open the door and all thoughts of what Lana might have been about to say disappears. Lori is waiting for me! The sight of her anxious face and unruly curls makes my heart sing.

"Hi," I say, grinning happily at her.

"Hello," she says shyly.

"Have you come to join my singing class?"

She nods.

I know I must look foolish, but I just can't stop grinning. "Fantastic. So you like singing?"

"Only in my room."

I laugh. "I do my best singing in the shower."

She smiles.

At that moment one of my other students comes in and immediately Lori's face changes. She stops smiling and drops her head. For the rest of the class she does not speak a word to anyone, and when the class is over she smiles at me quickly, and slips out of the room.

Seventeen

Sofia

When I come out to the foyer I see Lena talking to Jack and my stomach does a somersault. I straighten my shoulders and walk towards them.

My sister smiles and Jack gives me a head-to-toe look. His look makes me flush all over.

"Hello, Sofia," he says, his voice not full of desire like the last time we were together, but purely friendly.

"Lori came to my class," I blurt out.

"There you go. She couldn't keep away from you," he says with a twinkle in his eyes.

Kids from different classes and activities start pouring out of the corridor. They greet us casually by name and I experience the thrill of belonging. For the first time in my life I feel like a normal person. I'm not hiding in the castle, or being one of the whores in Valdislav's stable.

As they make their noisy exit through the front door, an awkward moment descends on our little group.

"Why don't you join us for dinner?" Lena suggests into the silence.

Jack glances at his watch. "Where're you guys going to?"

"Well, we were going to Sugar. My husband's running late so he will meet us there in about two hours," she says.

Jack looks sideways at me, his eyes veiled. "Sure," he agrees.

So we go off to Sugar and it is the strangest dinner I have ever had. The dynamics are weird. I don't taste a thing. My sister grills Jack unsuccessfully. Then Guy comes, and he is surprisingly cold towards Jack. And Jack? He just sits there, leaning back. Cool and totally unaffected by it all.

After dessert I excuse myself and go to the Ladies. In the mirror I see a woman who looks like a cornered rat. I try to remember Lena's saying. "Life is short. You have to grab it with both hands. Cake, shoes, and the man you want." The wind has loosened wisps of my hair. I pull them all back into my braid and go back out.

In the corridor I see Jack approaching. I stop and look behind me nervously. There is no one else around. He comes right up to me and stops in front of me. I retreat and he takes a step forward. I turn and press myself against the wall to let him pass and he cages me against it. His broad, muscular body completely blocks me off from sight, making me feel small and feminine. Brooding power and strength come off him in waves, but it doesn't fill me with fear.

It makes me want him more.

I want to climb him.

The only thing I fear is my own uncontrollable desire. I look up at him and our eyes lock. His are so dilated they are almost black. Images of our last encounter flood my mind. The sexual tension swirls like thick smoke around us. I feel a bolt of sensation flow through my body. It's desire. More than I ever thought possible. This man makes me feel things I have never felt before. The kind of passion I thought only existed in books.

He leans in until there is not even an inch between our faces. I can see a small white scar just under his right eyebrow. His breath fans my forehead. I should tell him that he needs to slow down. Take it easier, but I can hardly speak with the heat inside me.

"You look delectable tonight," he whispers, his sexy-as-hell mouth twisting.

"Thank you," I choke.

"Do you know you're fucking driving me crazy?"

My chest rises and falls rapidly. I lick my dry lips and he takes a deep breath and rests his forehead on mine.

"I want to see you with swollen lips after a whole night of kissing."

I gasp, a thrill of excitement flushing through my veins. "You shouldn't ..."

"No, I fucking shouldn't ..." he mutters to himself.

I swallow hard. "You're going too fast."

"Am I?" he growls.

His breath is warm and makes my whole body tingle. I want him so bad I can taste the need on my tongue. "Yes. We hardly know each other."

His eyes flicker. "I know everything I need to know about you."

His words are like a fast moving undercurrent that could pull me under.

"Sofia," a harsh voice calls.

The sensation that there is nobody else in the world but us shatters suddenly. I nearly jump out of my skin, but Jack doesn't turn immediately. He takes his time before turning to face the voice.

Guy's face is stern, his jaw clamped tight. I have never seen such an expression on his face. From the first day he found me he has always been gentle and kind with me. Completely ignoring Jack, he addresses me instead. "Your sister wants you."

With my face flaming, I straighten away from the wall and walk stiffly towards Guy. He throws another hard look at Jack before escorting me towards our table.

"Was he-"

"No," I say quickly before he can even finish his question.

"Are you all right?" he asks, his voice concerned.

"Yes." My whole body is still shivering with desire. "I'm fine."

He nods, but his forehead is creased with a deep frown.

When we get back to the table, Lena looks up at me with enquiring eyes. Slipping into my chair I smile tightly and shake my head to indicate that everything is all right. She turns to Guy and he looks deep into her eyes and gently rubs his thumb down her cheek. The gesture is so intimate and so full of profound love that I feel my stomach clench with a mixture of envy and longing.

After a few minutes Jack comes back, but he doesn't take his seat. He thanks Lena for inviting him and hopes we enjoy our dessert. Unfortunately, he has to leave since he has an early start in the morning, however he has taken care of the bill. I don't look at him even though I feel his eyes on me a few times.

"Goodnight, Sofia," he says, deliberately addressing me.

"Goodnight, Jack," I mumble, throwing him a quick glance.

His face is in shadow from the overhead lights, but his eyes watch me like a hunter. My fingers tighten around the edges of the table as I hurriedly drop my eyes down to my lap.

Shortly after Jack leaves we get into the car and make our way to the Kensington apartment. Irina is already in bed and her nanny wishes us goodnight before disappearing into her room.

Lena catches my arm. "Do you want to talk about it?" she asks.

"There's nothing to talk about," I say sadly.

"But he likes you," she implores.

I shake my head and run to my room. I can't talk about Jack to anyone. The sensations in my body are too raw to deal with right now. The truth is I am too cut about it. All this is too deep, too soon.

That night on my way to the toilet, I pass Guy and Lena's room and hear their whispering voices. Then I hear Lena crying and I know instantly that they are talking about me. The only thing in Lena's life that brings tears to her eyes is me and my condition. Guilt pours into my gut. I should have spoken to her when she wanted to. I'll speak to her now. I lift my hand to knock on their door, but I hear Guy's crooning voice try to soothe her, and my hand falls uselessly to the side of my body.

She will be all right. It will be all right.

Guy will make it all right for her. He always does.

There is one thing that is clear to me. I am bringing heartache and disharmony to the people I love the most. It is clear I cannot have him. I must face that and find a different way to be. Tomorrow I will tell Lena that I am not interested in Jack.

The next time I meet Jack I will apologize if I have given the wrong impression, but I am not available. The only relationship I am interested in is friendship. It's not like he will miss me too much. There must be loads of other women who want him. For a second the unwanted image of Fiona grasping Jack's hand fills my head.

Then I push it firmly out of my mind and continue on my way to the toilet.

Eighteen

Jack

I lied. I didn't have a damn place to be early in the morning. Surgery days are Tuesdays and Thursdays. This way I keep my surgery days when I need a steady hand and a clear head separate from my drinking days. I only have to be at work by mid-morning tomorrow.

I stalk out of the restaurant with my cock lighting up the inside of my pants. I've never wanted a woman the way I want her. With Lana it was mostly a deeply protective instinct. When I think back now it was purely brotherly for ages. In fact, until we were both adults it never even crossed my mind to think of her sexually. Even then it was tenderness and in a wildly romantic way. I dreamed of kissing her in the rain. I thought of myself as her knight in shining armor.

With Sofia I want to rip her sensible clothes off her and rut with her in the corridor of restaurants. I don't know what it is about her, but I'm mad for her. She says she's not interested but I know she wants it too. She feels the same pull. I have no idea where this crazy-mad desire comes from, but fucking hell it's stronger than me.

I hail a cab and give him the address of the pub. I shift in my seat to accommodate my erection. I lean back and think of Guy. Fuck, I had to stop myself from punching him one. Who the fuck does he think he is? Pompous prat. He should take care of the sister he's married to. The next time he gets in my way I won't be so polite. Actually, I'll wrench his head off his interfering neck.

The usual suspects are already clowning around at the bar.

"Hey, Tommy," I say dropping down into the last space around the table.

"Aren't ye a great little bastard?" he sings, more than half gone.

We drink steadily for the next couple of hours, but for the first time I don't get numb. I keep thinking about Sofia. The way she had looked up at me with tears in her eyes. It touched my heart. I can't even describe how beautiful she looked at that moment. I don't fucking want to be here. I want to be touching her, kissing her, pleasing her. Inside her.

Owning her.

Making her crave me.

The bell rings to indicate last orders. This is the time when the guys buy three rounds each so we can keep drinking long after drinking hours, but I stand up. Fuck, I'm unsteady on my feet, which means I've had even more than I thought.

"Where you off to?" Yann shouts drunkenly.

I raise my hand in a kind of farewell gesture and turn away. Weaving my way out of the pub, I push the door open. As I take my first lungful of freezing air, a man detaches himself from the shadows and comes up to me. I blink to clear my vision. Either I've drunk so fucking much I'm hallucinating, or Guy is standing in front of me.

"How did you know where I was?" I slur.

"Everybody knows where to find you on Tuesday, Friday, Saturday and Sunday nights, Irish," he says disgustedly.

Whoa: white fury. My scalp burns. He picked the wrong guy. On the wrong fucking night.

"I'm not here for a fight," he says.

"Well, you're going about it the wrong way then."

"My wife likes you, Irish, so I'm willing to accept that there might be a

 161

nice guy hidden somewhere inside the stupid drunk, but here's fair warning. I'm not going to let you hurt Sofia."

All my anger vanishes at his words. I blink stupidly at him. He thinks I'm going to hurt Sofia. What the fuck? "I'm not going to hurt her," I say, but it comes out so slurred even I can't make it out.

He shakes his head as if I revolt him and stabs his finger into my chest. My hand itches to grab his hand and break his fingers, but I resist the crazy urge. This is Sofia's brother-in-law.

"Look at you," he sneers. "You can barely stand. You've got everything, talent, looks, money, brains, fame, and you're just going to piss it all away in some low-life pub, aren't you?"

I slap his hand away. "Who the fuck do you think you are? God? This is my fucking life. If I want to piss it all away, what's it to you?"

"I'll tell you who the fuck I am. I'm Sofia's protector. You get that. Sofia's father, brother and uncle all rolled into one. You hurt one hair on her head, and I swear I'll destroy you. You have no idea what you're dealing with."

I start laughing. "Oh yeah?"

His jaw hardens and I see his hands clench into fists at his sides. "Don't play with her, Irish. She's not like other women. She's been through hell and back and if you're planning on leading her up the garden path, you better think again because I'll be damned if I stand by and watch a drunk like you soil a beautiful soul like her."

"I care about her," I shout.

He eyeballs me. "You don't care about anybody. How could you? You don't even care about yourself. You're an accident waiting to happen. One of these days, some guy's going to bury his knife in your chest, and it's going to be the end of Jack Irish. And pity anybody who loves you."

He's a big guy, but I'm a street fighter, and even pissed out of my head,

I can take him down. It will be a piece of cake, but I don't. He's saying and doing the things I should be doing for Sofia. She needs people like him to take care of her. I have a begrudging respect for him for taking the stand he has.

I collapse against the wall behind me. "Yeah, sure. I'll stay away from her."

"Yeah. I thought so," he mutters bitterly and turns away.

I want to call him back. I want to tell him I really care about Sofia, but he's right. Even totally smashed, I know he's right. I'm no good for her.

A man like me shouldn't even look at a woman like her. Someone like her needs a kind man. A man who is capable of love. Not someone without hope. Not the walking dead.

I look through the window into the pub. At all the other drunk men. They are laughing and talking loudly. But for the first time I see their unhappiness. Every one of them is a lost soul. Sure, they don't have my millions, but I am as lost as they are.

God, how did I come to be in this place?

I stand up unsteadily and stumble into the darkness.

Nineteen

Sofia

After my decision to have Jack in my life only as a friend I get some peace. Not as much as I'd hoped, but some. A part of me takes a step back and starts to think of him as an unattainable object. Like the Princes in the fables my mother read to us.

I spend my days with Mika and Irina and I go for long walks alone at dawn. A couple of times I go without shoes on the snow, but so long has passed since I did that with Master Yeshe I can no longer bear the cold and have to abandon the practice. That must have been a special time when I was a different person.

As I walk in the woods or fields leaving my footprints in the pristine snow, my heart never stops feeling heavy at the thought of giving Jack up. Sometimes I look towards the heavens, remember how far I have come, and try to feel grateful for everything I have. There is a little piece of wisdom Master Yeshe told me to tell myself when things got too difficult to handle.

This too will pass.

Every time my thoughts wander incessantly back to Jack, I repeat the four words like a mantra and to a certain extent it helps.

Finally, an eternity later, Thursday comes around. Just the thought of seeing him again makes my stomach twist, and I try to prepare myself for it by practicing all the different scenarios the meeting could take and the things I could say to him in each setting.

As we leave the house Lena takes my hands in hers and smiles at me encouragingly, her eyes are so pure and so full of love it actually makes my heart stop pumping so hard.

No matter what happens I'll have Lena.

Jack

It kills me not to turn up at the center on Thursday. It bothers me so bad I have to cancel all my appointments and take a last minute flight out of England. Ten hours later I land in sunny Nassau. My clothes start sticking to me even before I reach the air-conditioned taxi.

"Where to?" the driver asks.

"Surprise me," I tell him.

He laughs and puts his foot on the gas. The taxi lurches away from the curb. I love islanders. Say that to a British cab driver and he'll look at you as if you're mad. We drive by old colonial Georgian buildings in pastel colors, over two bridges, and stop in front of a dock.

The driver turns to me grinning broadly, his teeth gleaming whiter than a toothpaste advert.

"The boat will take you to Sivananda Yoga Ashram Retreat."

"What the?" I begin to say.

"You have no bag," he says by way of explanation.

I realize it is perfect. This is exactly what I need to recharge. I add a hefty tip to his fare and get out of the cab. Instantly I smell the salt in the sea breeze and know I have made the right decision.

When I arrive at the resort I am greeted by happy, helpful staff. It is considered low season and very quiet so I get an ocean front chalet with an amazing view of the beach. The peaceful energy of the place extends to my living accommodation. It is clean, the bed is comfortable, and the air conditioning works adequately.

I go for a swim in the gloriously azure sea. Floating in the calm water I can see groups of people meditating and others contorting into distressingly complicated yoga poses. Watching their serene faces I know that here I will detox the poisons from my soul and heal myself before I go back to claim my woman.

After a surprisingly good vegetarian meal of quinoa and roasted vegetables washed down with tea (at least that is what they call a cup of lukewarm water with a slice of orange and a couple of cloves thrown into it) I go to lay on the cool sand. As I listen to the steady sound of waves breaking on the beach, I come to a startling conclusion. I don't need healing. I don't need fucking anything. I already have everything I want.

All I need now is Sofia.

I take the boat out to the mainland and walk into a bar. It has a good lively atmosphere. Big fans everywhere, lots of tourists in colorful clothes, and a bustling waiting staff. I order a beer and it arrives with lovely condensation on the bottle. Even with all the fans it's still hot in the bar. I stare at it and think of my hand curling around the cold surface, the cool liquid slipping down my throat after the god awful "tea" from the canteen. I don't need it and I don't want it.

"It's a beer, not a snake," a heavily accented female voice says next to me.

I turn to look at her. Young, very young. Messy blonde curls. Tanned, friendly blue eyes, white shorts ... and long athletic legs. My money would be on an Australian backpacker out for a shoe-string night of free drinks and fun. Just the kind of girl I would have normally gone for.

"I wasn't sure. Thanks for the tip," I say, and start to walk out of the bar.

"If you're not having it, can I?" the blonde shouts over the noise.

"Knock yourself out, sweetheart," I call without turning around.

I know what I want and it is back home in England.

Twenty

Sofia

https://www.youtube.com/watch?v=ZN
r2XyEawig
(Unbreak My Heart)

It's impossible to describe my
disappointment when I finished my
class and opened the corridor door to
find Lena standing alone by the foyer
talking to Fiona. She turns to look at me
and straightaway she sees that I am
devastated. I know I told myself all week
that I didn't want to have a relationship
with him, that it would never work, I'd
only break my heart. But when he did
not turn up, my heart broke anyway.

For the rest of the week I go
through the motions. I walk, I talk, I eat,
but my whole being is waiting for
Thursday to come. I'm waiting for that

moment when my class will end and I walk down the corridor, open the door, and see Jack standing there in work clothes, telling me he's starving and asking if I want to join him for a burger at his friend's café.

Then Thursday comes. I dress in a black top, blue jeans, black boots and an oversized coat. It's a modern, trendy look. Lena can carry it off no problem, but I don't know that I have.

Anyway, Lori doesn't turn up and I take it as a bad omen. When my class ends and my students leave, I put on my coat, gather my things, and begin to walk down the corridor.

For the first time it seems endless.

I reach the door and my heart is like a stone in my chest. It doesn't matter if he is not there, I tell myself. It's not the end of the world. It'll probably be a blessing in disguise. It was always wrong anyway. I lift my hand and push the door. It swings open and I walk through it.

Oh. My. God.

He's there. Talking to Lena. He is laughing at something she said. When the door swings open he lifts his head and looks straight at me. And smiles. There is something different about him. My knees are like jelly. His eyes travel down my body. I'm so happy my heart feels as if it will jump right out of my chest.

His eyes never leave me as I walk to him.

"Hey," he says softly.

I can't speak. I smile a stupid, happy, crazy grin.

"You hungry?" he asks.

I nod, still too overwhelmed to speak.

Suddenly I become aware that my sister's mouth is next to my ear.

"I'll go back with Guy now and I'll send Robert to pick you up from the apartment tomorrow at lunchtime, okay?"

For a second her words don't make sense and I stare at her with surprise. Then it hits me. This is going to be my first night of independence. I'll be like any other woman on a date with a man. She wants me to have choices. I can say goodnight to him at the door or invite him in for coffee.

My sister holds my gaze, her eyes steady and strong. God, I love my sister so much it makes me want to cry to think that I am always the cause of unhappiness in her life. I smile at her. I make my smile confident and carefree. I'll be fine, my smile says. Slowly she smiles back.

I love you, she mouths in Russian.

Me too, I mouth back in Russian.

Then she turns to Jack. "Well, I should be going. You will take care of my Sofia, won't you?" Her voice trembles.

"With my life," Jack tells her.

She nods. Wrought with emotion she turns away blindly and heads towards the entrance. The door closes on her as I watch.

"She has nothing to worry about. I'll never hurt you," Jack says softly.

I look up at him. His eyes are intense and serious. He has no idea how much I hope and pray that is true.

"Come on," he says, his hand on the small of my back gently guiding me in the direction of the door. As we get out I see Lena sitting in the backseat, the car is turning away, and she is staring ahead, lost in thought.

"Where are we going?" I ask as we walk towards Jack's car.

"You'll see," he says mysteriously.

He parks the car on the same street as before and we walk up the road. He doesn't hold my hand, but it is obvious we are together by the looks of the women who pass us by. They look at him then their eyes slide down to me. After a while I start to glow with pride and happiness. I can't believe that a hunk like Jack would actually want to go out with me.

We walk past his friend's burger place. I look through the glass window and see that it is empty. The waitress is sitting on a table laughing while Paddy speaks animatedly and gestures with his long limbed body. We carry on down the road until Jack comes to a stop in front of McDonalds.

I laugh. "Seriously?"

"Yeah. I'll poison myself for you," he says, and pulls open the door.

It is empty but for a table with two young girls who seem to be already mothers with prams pushed up to their table and another table with kids still in their school uniforms.

They wave at Jack and he smiles and nods back. We walk up to the counter and join the shortest queue. There is only one person ahead of us. I steal a glance at him and he is looking up at the menu with a I-don't-believe-I'm-doing-this look on his face. It's actually a very sexy look, but it also makes me want to giggle. As the server rings up the customer's order I poke Jack in his stomach. It's like poking wood!

"Last chance to back out," I tease.

He looks down at me and grins. "Don't worry about me. At least I'll die happy."

Like a fool I go a horrible shade of red, the burn blasting up my neck and into my cheeks.

His eyes twinkle with amusement.

"Can I help you?" the cashier asks.

Awkwardly, I take the two steps that bring me to the counter.

The server looks bored. "What can I get you today?"

"A cheese burger, one chicken McNuggets, one large fries, an Oreo McFlurry and a strawberry Milkshake."

"And what about you, Sir?"

"A Big tasty, medium fries, side salad, and a Coke," he says.

Our food is loaded onto two trays and we carry it to a table in a corner.

I survey all the packages in front of me with satisfaction. From now on when someone talks about getting a McDonalds I'll know what they're talking about.

Twenty-one

Jack

I watch her surveying all the packages in front of her with a child's delight, and I want to hunt down and kill those people who hurt her. How could anyone even think of hurting such an innocent and vulnerable creature? I understand why her sister and Guy guard and protect her almost obsessively.

Her delicate hands reach for the little cartons of sauces first. She has ordered three different types and she peels the tops off them and lays them in a row on the table. Then she opens the box of chicken nuggets.

"Bon appetite," I say softly, curious to see how she plans to fit all this food into her tiny body.

"Same to you," she says. With a grin she takes the first piece, dips it in the sauce and delicately bites into it, and what do you know, my cock goes rock hard. This is new for me. I've never reacted this way to anyone before. Shit. Shifting in my seat I watch her open the burger next and take it in her hands.

"Aren't you going to eat?" she asks me.

I take a bite of my burger. For plastic it tastes quite good.

She dips a French fry into ketchup and slips it into her mouth. Then she breaks the straw out of its packaging and sticks it into the milkshake. She sucks at the straw. Here we go again. I watch her lush lips release the straw, her tongue come up and lick her lips. Like a woman on a mission she opens the ice cream and dips her plastic spoon into it. She licks the spoon. Fuck, this is the meal from hell. I'm so desperately hard I'm going to need to go and relieve myself in the toilet.

She sighs contentedly. "I'm done," she says.

I raise my eyebrows. "What? You've only had a taste of everything you've ordered."

"Well, after you said what you did about McDonalds I went and did some research and you're absolutely right."

I lean back, surprised and amused.

"See this bun here. You'll never believe the long list of chemicals that are in it. It's actually painted with mold inhibitors. Not only have I eaten preservatives, dextrose, sodium phosphate, but also a variety of ingredients used for making flame retardant material, yoga mats, safety matches and contact explosives."

She never stops surprising me. "So why did you want to come in here?"

She shrugs. "I wanted to know what I was missing and now I do."

"Did you like it?"

"Well, I didn't hate it, but I prefer your friend's burger." She reaches out her hand and touches my arm and I burn. "Thank you for bringing me here. I really appreciate it. Now can we go somewhere else, please?"

I laugh. Standing, I pull her up and grab her by the hips so she is pulled close to me. She gasps and looks up at me. She is too thin. I feel the tiny bones push into my body. Otherwise she's goddamn perfect. I want to take her back to my place, tangle my body with hers, and fuck until my cum drips from her fucked pussy.

"Fuckin' get a room," one of the kids shouts.

Don't worry kid that's not how I'm gonna play this. I'm going to take it easy with her. I rub my thumb against her cheek. "Let's go get some proper food."

We end up in an Italian joint. It's really old fashioned with burnt sienna and yellow walls and bottles of Frascati and ham hanging from the rafters. I know the owner. Salvatore is jolly and round. Sometimes he takes his guitar out and sings corny old Italian songs. He's not very good, but his customers don't mind. There's something sweet about his singing. While he is singing you can pretend you have gone back in time. You are sitting in a trattoria in Italy.

We sit sipping Salvatore's best Gavi de Gavi while we wait for our spaghetti vongole. Today's special.

"So you grew up in Russia?"

Almost instantly I feel her shrink. "Yes, we grew up in Russia," she says woodenly.

I change the subject. From then on we stay away from the past. I ask her about her taste in music. Oh dear, she likes classical. She asks me for mine. I tell her I like techno. She loves chocolate ice cream. I don't. She doesn't like curry and I could live on it. She likes River Dance and I think they look like puppets jerking around. She likes mountains. I like beaches. I love watching a good boxing match, she cannot bear any kind of sport that involves violence.

Our clam spaghetti arrives. We dig in. I ask her to tell me the person she would most want to have dinner with.

"Dead or alive?" she asks.

"Either."

She names Princess Diana.

"Why?"

"I'd like to ask her what really happened that night."

"Don't you believe the official story then?"

She drops her voice to a whisper. "No."

I hide a smile. My date is a secret conspiracy theorist.

She asks me the same question. I don't need to think about this one.

"You," I say, and I really mean it too. I'd like to have dinner with her and find out the great secret she is hiding. Why she thinks she is so unloveable.

"Me?" she asks.

"Yeah, you."

We stare at each other. Her eyes look gold. Some great hurt shines in them. Then the waiter comes to refill our glasses and it is gone.

I ask for her favorite color.

"Blue," she says, a smile coming back to her eyes. "You?"

I smile. "Blue."

"Oh my God. I can't believe it. We finally found something we agree about."

Salvatore starts singing. Her eyes become misty. We have dessert. Creamy tiramisu. I watch her eat it and feel my gut tighten. This is my girl. I'm never stopping until I make her mine. For life. We order coffee. Salvatore brings flaming Sambucas with them. We blow out the flames and down them. She laughs. There is color in her cheeks and her eyes are shining.

"More coffee?" I ask, my hands hungry to roam her flesh.

She nods happily.

As we leave she stumbles against me. I grab her slim waist and steady her. She looks up at me.

"Thank you. This has been the best night of my life," she whispers.

Twenty-two

Sofia

https://www.youtube.com/watch?v=Z7oPHkqzPqA

I so very nearly ask Jack to come up.

Well, it will be an outright lie to say anything else as there is no time during our date that my body does not clamor for his.

When he pulls me into his arms outside the lift and kisses me with desperate hunger, it is like being pulled into quicksand. It takes all of my willpower to break the kiss and press the button for my floor.

As the lift door closes on him, my skin, flesh, bones, blood, and sinew all scream for him. But another part of me ... a frozen part ... the part that holds

together the rickety structure of sanity ... the one that never once got merry with alcohol, or drunk with sexual desire, says, *don't spoil the best night of your life.*

Let the magic be ruined another day.

Let this night be special.

I ride the lift up to the apartment alone and put my key in the door. It is strange and empty without Lena, Guy and Irina, but I don't mind. I'm floating on a delicious cloud. I dance into the room, switch on lights, and put on music, Beethoven's Fifth. Humming and pretending to play an invisible violin to the lively music, I make my way into the bathroom. I finish my toilette, change into my long cotton nightgown, and fall dreamily into bed.

Am I falling in love?

Something that would have been impossible only a short while ago. I stare at the ceiling, confused. That word that I read about in books and only happened to other people. I've known only pain. And yet, it must be. What else could be so perfect, so wonderful, so amazing? I fall asleep on that lovely cloud.

The doorbell jerks me out of a deep and dreamless sleep. I freeze with fear, my eyes swiveling to the luminous face of my alarm clock. It is nearly twelve o'clock. I squeeze my eyes shut. Don't panic. No one but Jack and my family know I'm here. Obviously it's just a mistake by someone, or it could be someone drunk ringing the wrong bell. They will go away. There is nothing to fear.

The doorbell goes again. This time more insistent.

I bite my thumbnail nervously. What if it is a woman who has lost her keys and just needs to be let in out of the cold? I hesitate another few seconds and the bell goes again.

This time I get out of bed and quickly walk to the hallway. If it's a stranded woman I'll let her in. If it's a man I'll pretend there's no one at this address. Without switching on any lights, I go to the intercom and turn on the video. For a couple of seconds, I think I must be hallucinating. Then my entire body tenses, not with fear, but with unadulterated excitement. Jack's come for me. I press the answer buzzer.

"What are you doing, Jack?" I ask, my voice strangely breathless.

"Let me in," he demands, swaying slightly.

"Are you drunk?"

"What do you think?" he asks.

"I think, yes," I say cautiously.

His hair flops over his forehead and he sweeps it out of the way carelessly and claps his hands. "Bravo. Let me in so I can give you your prize," he slurs.

Even drunk he looks awesome. I want him to come up so bad my body aches, but how can I? There are so many reasons I shouldn't. Not least my disfigured skin. My intolerably ugly scars. If he sees my back in the condition he is in, he won't be able to hide his revulsion. Everything will fall apart.

"I think you should go home, Jack," I whisper.

"I don't want to go home, Sofia. Let me in. Please. Just this once."

Something inside me lurches painfully. "I can't," I cry.

"We don't have to do anything. I just want to talk."

My breath comes out in a gasp. "Talk?"

"Yeah. You can make me a coffee and help me to sober up before I drive home."

I take a deep breath. I wouldn't leave a dog out in this weather let alone Jack. "Promise?"

"Scouts honor."

I press the buzzer and watch him push open the door. I switch on the light and quickly run to the mirror. I had pulled my hair into a braid at the side of my head before I went to bed. It looks messy. Strands hang on either side of my face. I quickly swipe them back and tuck them behind my ears. I rub my eyes to make them look more awake and pull together the front of my nightgown. I don't want to encourage something I'm not ready for.

I jump when I hear the knock on the door. Wow, he was fast.

Too fast to have waited for the elevator. He must have run up the stairs. I twist the handle and take a step back.

Oh my! Jack outside on the street is one thing. Jack looming in my hallway is completely another matter.

Before I can say a word he takes a step forward and pulls me into his arms. Taken completely by surprise I tumble into his broad chest. Almost instantly I feel myself losing my composure, unraveling. His body is hard and unyielding. Oh sweet Jesus, this is exactly what I did not want to happen.

"You said … talk … coffee," I croak.

"Fuck talking and coffee, Sofia. I came here for a taste of your sweet body."

The fumes of alcohol on his breath hit my nostrils, but it doesn't put me off in the least. I want this man inside me. Where did this desire for a man come from? I've never wanted a man in my life, never even imagined I might want to, let alone this bad. He puts one big, warm man arm under my back and the other under my knees and lifts me up. So close to his neck I get a whiff of his cologne.

"Tonight I'm going to ravish you. Make you mine," he growls possessively into my ear.

I feel his breath fan the top of my hair as he carries me down the hallway towards the only open door. My bedroom. He takes me inside and lays me on the bed. My heart is galloping in my chest.

I look up at him as he towers over me. In dim light from the corridor his face is full of shadows, hard. I can't tell his expression, but his eyes glitter hotly. My mind snaps this image as the precious moments before our love affair ends.

I put off telling him the truth about me for so long because I didn't want to see this searing lust die away, to be replaced by disgust. For the first time in my life I was enjoying the attention, the feeling of being wanted, desired. Tonight, in the next few minutes it will all come to an end.

He reaches for me.

"I need to tell you something first," I say. My voice is oddly calm.

"You can tell me after I've had you," he says curling his hand around my ankle.

"No," I insist. "It's important. I have to tell you this first. Then you decide if you still want to have me."

He releases my ankle, his eyes narrowing. "Go on. Spit it out."

I can already feel tears burning the backs of my eyes, but I harden my heart. I'll tell him and he'll run a mile, but it'll be all right. I'll survive this tragedy exactly the way I've survived everything else.

Baby steps.

It was fun while it lasted.

Lifting my body off the bed, I scoot away from him on my hands and butt. When my back touches the headboard I wrap my arms around my body and start speaking. "When I was young my father sold me to a trafficking gang."

His jaw drops. Even in the darkness I can see his body go slack with shock. He blinks and stares at me in disbelief.

"The gang sold me to a brothel owner in Brussels. For many years," my voice breaks, but I clear my throat and carry on, "I lived with him and serviced his clients. Mostly politicians. You know, members of the European Parliament. They were away from their wives and they needed company."

Oh God, why am I babbling like a fool? I can't believe I'm telling him about the men who came to abuse me. White-washing them. They needed company! I take a deep breath. Quick. *Cut to the chase, Sofia.*

"Then a year ago Guy rescued me and brought me to live with him and Lena in Cheshire." I exhale. "Christmas Eve last year was my first social outing."

He drops to his knees. Like an elephant felled by a hunter in a long range gun. Defeated by something he could never fight. Something he never saw coming. Up this close I see his eyes and they are full of horror. Dumbfounded horror.

I force a smile. "So if you want to leave now, go ahead. I'll totally understand."

At the sound of my voice he holds his head and shakes it as if to clear it, or as if he can't process the information I have given him. I gaze at him silently.

"Oh, fuck," he roars suddenly, and his voice is so full of fury I jump. He turns his body to the side and violently slams his fist on the floor. He keeps on slamming it and a frisson of fear runs up my spine. He is going to hurt himself.

"Stop," I scream.

As quick as lightning he scrambles up on the bed, grabs my leg, and pulls me towards him so my feet land on the ground and he ends up kneeling between my thighs. He grasps my upper arms. "And you were frightened to tell me this because you thought I would turn tail and run. What the fuck, Sofia?"

My heart starts racing, not with fear, but with exhilaration and hope. I damp it down. There is worse to come.

"I didn't know what to think. It's enough to make any man run," I breathe.

"Not this one," he snarls.

I take a shuddering breath. No point dragging it out. "There's one more thing I have to show you."

He releases my arms. "Go on," he grates.

I take my gown off and turn around.

"What the fuck is that?" I hear him ask incredulously.

I whirl my head and face him. He looks like he is going to pass out or puke. I press my bunched up nightgown against my naked breasts.

"He ... branded me."

"With his name?" he asks, as if unable to believe what he is hearing.

I nod slowly.

He buries his face in his hands. "Oh. Fuck. Fuck. Fuck. No matter where I go, I can't. I just can't fucking run away from the cruelty of human beings." His voice is hoarse, suffering. I almost don't recognize it.

I reach out a hand towards his bent head. I don't touch him. I just hover it inches away from his silky hair. His hands are clenched and his whole body is trembling with fury and incredible pain.

I watch as his silent tears drip on the floor.

My pain has become his, and he can't take it. I feel a wave of love for the tortured man. He doesn't deserve to suffer like this. I touch his head gently.

And he looks up slowly as if he is seeing me for the first time.

Twenty-three

Sofia

"It's okay," I whisper, wiping away his tears. "I know you can't stomach it. I understand. Like I said before. We'll be friends. We'll always be friends. You can go home and we'll forget this ever happened. We'll pretend this night never happened."

It seems forever that he gazes into my eyes. Then he sighs, the sound loud in the silence of my bedroom. "I don't need to go home, Sofia. I'm in the right place," he says.

My mind goes blank with shock. "Are you sure?"

"You're it for me. Wherever you are is exactly where I'm meant to be."

I stare at him in astonishment. A thousand times I dreamed of this moment, but it was never this

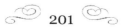

passionate, determined declaration. Never. Tears well up in my eyes.

"Don't, my sweet child. Don't," he croons.

I blink hard. I don't want to cry. I let go of all my fears. I don't want him to think of me as a child. I want to be his woman. Strong, sexy, desirable.

He sits on the floor and pulls me down onto his lap. I hold onto his shoulders and straddle his thighs. He pulls my hair tie, unbraids my hair, and fluffs it out so it halos my face.

"Exactly how I thought you'd look. Beautiful. Just beautiful." His face is flushed with desire. This is it. This is the moment I didn't dare dream. Valdislav took too much from me, but he could never have my heart. That was always mine, but tonight I give it freely to this fine man.

"I don't have a condom," I murmur.

"I have, but I don't want to use one with you."

My eyes widen. "Why?"

"We'll use it if you want to, but I want to fill you with my cum. I want to coat the outside and inside of your body with me. With my smells, my seed, my sweat, my blood if necessary. I want you to be my woman. I want to obliterate the memory of any other man. From today there will be no other for you but me."

"What if I get pregnant?"

"Then we'll find a name for our baby."

My eyes get big. "You want to have a baby with me?"

He smiles. "I can't think of better a mother than you."

I stare at him in amazement. For as long as I can remember all I ever wanted was my own little family, but after what happened to me I pushed the thought away as something impossible, and yet this ... this is too good to be true. I'm not one of those lucky people who have good things happening to them all the time.

"Are you sure?" I gasp.

"I've been a fool most of my life. I crammed twenty lifetimes into my life and nothing made me happy. I know what I want. I want you."

I'm almost afraid I am dreaming, that I will wake up in the morning and find myself alone in bed. That it has all been just a dream. I drop my eyes in total confusion and my gaze falls on the hard bulge in his pants.

The sight transports me to the past.

For years I spent my days and nights in sexual mode. In fact, I didn't know any other way to be. From the time I was sold Valdislav groomed me to be a sexual being. I had to perform, or I was punished. It was normal for me to give a blowjob, or have sex on demand at any time of the day or night.

For the last year I fought to forget all that. I never wanted another man in my body. I wore dowdy, loose-fitting clothes, and never made eye contact with men. I became the opposite of what I was. I became a sexless being, and I was happy being that. I felt clean. I felt good.

But one look at Jack's erection, and a switch goes off in my head, and suddenly I'm back in sexual mode. I reach for his belt. I know what men like and I know exactly how to give it to them.

"Let me get you off. I'm real good at this."

His hand instantly covers mine.

My eyes fly up to his. "What is it?"

His eyes are glowing with something fierce and animal-like. He shakes his head. "Everything that has happened to you until now was a mistake. You were not just made for getting cocks off. You were made for me, Sofia Seagull," he whispers. He kisses my ears, my neck, making my head fall back with pleasure. "You were made for this, Princess Sofia," he says, catching my bottom lip between his teeth.

Our eyes are so close there are only a couple of inches between us. His are heavy-lidded and so dark they are bottomless black pits.

He sucks at my bottom lip.

"And this."

He brushes his fingertips on my nipples.

A shiver goes down my spine.

He bends his head and kisses the hardened tip of my breast.

I gasp.

"Tonight and every night I'm going to kiss and suck every fucking inch of you," he says, and takes the nipple into his mouth.

My body responds instantly and between my legs I become a sopping wet mess.

He reaches behind him and pulls out something tucked into his jeans.

"You carry a knife around?" I gulp.

"Sorry, old habit,' he mutters.

I stare at him curiously. The light from the corridor flashes on the blade as he unsheathes it. If it had been anyone else I would have been frightened. Frightened … I would have run a mile.

But this is Jack. Jack with the straight black hair and the sad smile. Jack whose body I have dreamed of and craved. Jack, who saw my burnt flesh and cried for me. Jack wanting me to expose myself to his blue, blue eyes. Excitement runs through me. I do. I want him to see me naked.

"Don't move," he commands and I freeze.

Our gazes lock. Juices gush out of me. Cold steel slides under my panties. I never thought I would ever give this much control to a man again. He cuts through it cleanly, then slices the other side too. The scrap of material falls away. He tosses the knife behind him and looks down between my splayed thighs. Automatically, instinctively, my hands move to cover myself. He lays his hand over mine and rubs the thumb of his other along my jaw.

"I just need to look at you, baby," he says, his voice thick.

I swallow. "This is a huge moment for me, Jack. I want you, but I'm scared."

"If you want to go slow, if you need a bit more time, I'll wait, I can be patient. I'll do whatever it takes, but understand this, I'm never going away."

For long moments we simply stare at each other then I nod slowly.

Grasping my hands and holding them both at the wrists he lifts them high above my head. Now I am even more exposed and vulnerable. I look into his eyes. They are dark and watching. Fierce. Intense. Scary. Nothing like what they normally look like.

He pulls the wet scrap of material trapped between his thighs and me and flings it away. I sit as naked as the day I was born on his lap. Supporting my back with his other hand he lays me flat on the floor. The polished wood is cold on my back.

"Spread your legs and let me see your sweet cunt," he orders.

My legs feel rubbery. Nervously, I part my legs and watch his eyes move down my body to my exposed sex. I see him drink in the sight of my nakedness. Then he smiles. Slowly. With great satisfaction. Sensuously he runs his hands up and down my body.

"You're not a prostitute. You're flawless and ... you're mine."

I close my eyes. This has to be a dream. The most beautiful man in the world is telling me I am his. Me, the dirty prostitute.

He lays his large warm hand on my pussy and rests it there. Possessively. His eyes lock on mine as the heat from his hand seeps into my cold flesh. My pussy starts to really cream, wet his hand, drip. It's all too much. I close my eyes.

"Sofia," he whispers.

I open my eyes.

Bending his head, he *breathes* in the scent of my arousal. No one has ever done that to me. I moan softly.

"How long I've waited for this sweet scent. I even wanted our first kiss to be my mouth on this sugar cunt."

Softly he kisses the heated skin of my mound. My hips rise off the floor in anticipation. He drags his lips down lower and I want to scream with the wild sensation of his velvet lips.

"My first taste," he says, and spreading my labia with his fingers, licks the wet seam. His tongue is like a trail of fire.

"Oh, Jack," I moan as my hips jerk and writhe helplessly.

He slips a thick finger into me.

My mouth opens in shock. It's been two years since anyone has touched me. I read about other women who pleasure themselves with their fingers and vibrators, but I have never done it. The idea of sex is wrapped with disgust and degradation for me. Yet here I am starving for his finger, his tongue, his cock.

"How wet you are," he purrs, letting his finger glide lazily in and out of me.

Then I watch him bury his face between my open legs.

"Mmm,' he says. His next words are mumbled into my throbbing flesh and not only do I hear them but I feel their vibration. "I want you to cum in my mouth. I want your cum running down my throat and chin."

I feel my sex pulsing as he eats me, no, that is too tame a word for what he does. He devours me, as if he can't get enough of me, or hasn't eaten for days. I think he will tire soon, but the more he feasts, the more ravenous he gets. My tense body bows completely off the floor, every nerve ending buzzing, ready for something big.

Suddenly, for the first time in my life, I climax. It is a powerful flash of heat that comes from nowhere and hits

me so hard and deep it shatters me. As it ebbs away and my body stops clenching and jerking I stare at him in awe. My arms feel weak and my thighs are trembling.

"That's my first orgasm," I pant.

His eyes widen with surprise. Then he surprises me.

"And here's your second one, baby," he says, dipping his tongue back into my throbbing sex.

Twenty-four

Jack

https://www.youtube.com/watch?v=ZJ
L4UGSbeFg
(Man I Feel Like A Woman Tonight)

I get lost in her smell and heat. Only after her thighs clench uncontrollably and she screams with ecstasy do I reluctantly lift my head and look at her.

Goddamn it, she's indescribably beautiful.

Lying on the floor, her long silky hair spread out around her, her chest rising and falling fast. Fresh. Young. Innocent. I cannot even begin to get my head around the idea of her being anything other than an angel come down to tempt me.

"Oh my God," she whispers.

I wipe my mouth with the back of my hand and, bending forward, lift her. She is too thin. No one but a child should weigh this little. I'll get the curves back on her. Carefully, I place her on the bed, exactly on the narrow rectangle of light coming from the doorway.

My dick is rock hard. Ready to fuck.

I pull my shirt off and unbuckle my belt. It feels as if I've been waiting all my life for this moment.

"I want you to open your legs as wide as you can. Spread them wide, Sofia, so I can see all that belongs to me. And only me."

She hesitates, then nervously obeys. I remember our first kiss. My blood had raged for her then, but it is nothing compared to how desperate I am for her now. I want to drop to my knees and bury my cock in her pussy and tell her that she belongs to me only. I flick open the fly of my jeans.

"That's it, baby. All mine," I growl, looking at her gorgeous cunt. Her flesh is swollen and glistening in the narrow rectangle of light. Out, open, and begging me to fuck it. Beautiful.

I yank my pants down and kick them away from me. My cock bounces with desire.

"Fuck. Look at your pussy. It wants to be taken. You want my cock in your pussy, baby?"

She nods eagerly, but if I allow myself to get into that sweet body I'm going to blow in record time. Nah, I want to hear her scream again. I climb on the bed. On my knees in front of her open pussy I stroke myself. Three strokes, a record for me, and I'm fucking gone, spurting warm seed onto her stomach.

Her delicate hands drift away from the bed. Slowly, in large sensuous circles, she rubs my cum into her skin as if it is luxurious body cream. There is so fucking much she smooths it into her hips, her waist, her breasts, and her neck. Then with her eyes fixed on me she pushes her semen coated finger into her pussy.

My dick becomes rock solid again.

"Believe it or not you're the only woman I've ever been this greedy for," I say, and diving between her legs, eat her sweet cunt for the third time.

Her hands reach out, grabbing my hair, pulling my face into her groin. I've taught her well. She knows that I'm here to give freely. Hungrily, I open my mouth and suck that whole peachy pussy into it.

I fucking can't get enough of her.

Twenty-five

Sofia

Even though I am exhausted I am too excited to fall back to sleep. I close my eyes, safe inside the warmth and security of his arms, and I wait until his breathing becomes deep and even. Then I watch him for hours, unable to believe that such a magnificent man could want me this way. It seems too incredible.

When it is nearly morning I carefully slip out of bed and cover my nakedness. My whole body feels tense and restless as I stand over him. What will he be like when he wakes up sober? I don't have long to wait.

He opens his eyes suddenly, almost in a panic. One moment they are closed and all is serene and still, the next his eyes are wide open and wild, and he is jack-knifing off the bed. I am too shocked to move. His eyes collide with mine, relief crosses his face, and he falls back onto the pillows.

"Did you have a bad dream?" I ask.

"Yeah." He holds his hand out and I entwine my fingers through his. Mine are trembling.

"Do you have a hangover?"

"The only hangover I have is for your juicy pussy," he says, his eyes closed, his mouth lifting up in a small smile. "Your smell is driving me insane."

I blush madly. "So you do remember everything we did yesterday?"

His eyes open and he pulls me towards him. Catching me by my waist he lifts me back on the bed. He kicks the bedsheets away from his naked body. His erection is massive. He tugs my nightgown over my head and stares at my naked body.

"Sit on my face," he orders.

With my knees on either side of him I walk up his body until I reach his

mouth. Slowly I lower my sex over his mouth. He sucks and licks my pussy, and pushes his tongue in as far as it will go. Gently he nibbles the tender hood of my clit before clamping it with his whole mouth and sucking until I climax uncontrollably.

Grabbing my hips, he lifts me away from his mouth and says, "Now put my cock inside you."

I grab the base of it and bring it to my opening. Staring boldly into his eyes I tease the tip of his cock on the lips of my wet sex.

"Fuck, Sofia. You're killing me," he groans.

And I smile. I have never had power. Not ever. Always everybody else controlled me, my body, my actions. For the first time in my life I feel powerful. Because of this man.

Jack

I run my hands greedily up her thighs, reveling in the smoothness. There are faint scars on the insides of them, but on the front, outsides and back they are like the finest silk. I look at her pale body rising over me and she is like a mirage. A shining patch of water in the arid desert that I have lived in for years. I still can't believe I am in her bed.

We didn't use a condom last night. And I don't regret it. In fact, I'm glad. Nothing should ever come between us.

I bend forward and bite the nymph's nipple.

I want to leave my mark on her body. I want to brand her. I want to forget that abomination on her back. She is mine. Only mine. No matter what it says on her back. She is MINE. MINE. MINE.

She fists my bare cock and starts to impale her hot, tight pussy down on it.

Pure heaven. I don't let go of her nipple. I suck it hard, and she groans as my cock travels deeper and deeper into her body. I know she must be sore from all the hard fucking last night, and I know it's kind of primitive and uncivilized of me, but that is exactly how I want her. Sore and ruined for any other man.

That's what I did. I fucked her rough and claimed her for me. For Jack Irish. She tries to lift herself off me. I grab hold of her hips and push all the way home.

She screams.

"You want this?" I grunt, pushing up again.

Her eyes snap to mine as her pussy clamps involuntarily. "Yes."

I thrust hard. Yup. I get in there. Deep. I thrust even harder. Rougher. She begins to climax. Her legs are wide open and I have a front seat view to her orgasm. She clenches my cock and starts cumming hard on me. Her pussy spurting and gushing as I continue to fuck her. My shaft glistens with her juices. Just seeing her lose control makes me lose it. I'm gonna cum inside her again. I'm gonna fill her up.

I thrust one last time and empty into her womb.

I cum hard and it feels as if I'm unloading a shitload of sperm into her. I keep her plugged up for a few seconds while I lazily move my cock in and out of her. Then I ask her to lift herself above me and I watch my cum slowly drip out of her cunt in long strings. And ... it's a fucking beautiful sight.

Sofia

The way he watches me makes me bold and alive. As if I am intensely wanted. As if I am something precious. I've never been anything but a place where a man can slake his lust. This hole would do just as well as the other.

"Come here," he says. I know he wants me to lie on his body. The first thought in my head is, his arms are going to go around me and he's going to feel the uneven ridges of my scars. I reach for my nightgown. His hand reaches out and flings it out of the way.

"Why are you hiding from me?" he asks, frowning.

I shake my head.

He stares at me for a moment longer then he says, "Don't."

I just look at him.

"Turn around."

"No," I breathe. It would ruin what we just had. I'd rather he never saw it again. It was night before, it's day now and light is creeping in through the shutters. It looks far worse in the day.

He places his hands around my waist, and his eyes glitter with a strange light. "Everything that is on your body belongs to me. That scar is mine too. Now show me my scar," he orders, his voice steely.

For a few seconds I hold his unblinking gaze, then I turn around and close my eyes. His fingers touch my back and I jump. Slowly his fingers trace the letter N. Every muscle in my body becomes as taut as a guitar string.

"Relax," he says, one of his hands curled firmly around my upper arm while a finger from his other hand finds the deep crease of the letter i. I want him to stop.

"Leave it," I blurt out, jerking my body away, but not being able to move far because of his firm hold on my arm.

"Why? It's just a scar. A bit of burnt skin and flesh."

"He made me hideous. I hate him," I cry.

His finger follows the curl of the next letter. "It's only ugly if you think it is. He has no power over you. You are mine now and no man will lay a fucking finger on you while there is breath left in my body."

I begin to sob.

He turns me around, and lifting off the pillows, he holds me tight. "Do you want me to remove it for you?"

I stop sobbing and stare at his kind eyes in disbelief. "You can remove it?" My voice is hoarse, shocked. I pull away from him. It has never even crossed my mind that such a big and ugly thing could be removed. I thought I would have to live with it forever.

"Yes. I will turn his name and memory into little scars that will fade with time until you can hardly see them."

"Yes. Yes, I want that. Very much," I cry.

He smiles. "I will schedule your surgery for next week."

I hug him tightly. I can't even believe something so wonderful could happen to me.

The phone ringing startles me. The outside world still exists.

"That will be Lena," I say. "I better answer it or she will worry like mad."

Twenty-six

Sofia

He lets go of me and I run out of the room buck naked. Yesterday such a thing could never have happened. I pick up the phone and say a breathless hello.

"Good morning," Lena says.

"Hi," I say.

"Did you have a good time last night?" she asks.

"Yes, it was lovely," I say.

There is a brief silence, then Lena says, "He's still there, isn't he?"

"Yes," I admit, my heart bubbling over with happiness.

"Are you happy?" Her voice is oddly expressionless, as if she is afraid of my answer.

"Yes, yes, I am," I say quickly.

She sighs. "Oh, Sofia. I love you so much."

"Me too," I say, my eyes flooding with new tears. "Lena, I've got something to tell and show you when I see you."

"What is it?" she asks, her voice instantly flooding with anxiety.

"It's not a bad thing. I thought it was, but it's not. It's all okay."

"Are you sure?" she asks uncertainly.

"Yes, I'm very sure."

"What time do you want me to send Rodger to pick you up?"

"Can I call you back after I have spoken to Jack?"

"Okay. Just call on my mobile because I have to pop into the village soon. Do you want anything from there?"

"No." There is not a thing I can think of at the moment except Jack in my bed waiting for me.

"How about one of those cream cakes from the bakery?"

"Okay," I say with a laugh.

"Chocolate or strawberry?"

"Chocolate."

"All right then. Call me when you know."

"I will. Lena?"

"Yeah."

"Did Mika miss me last night?"

"Badly. She refused to stop crying. I had to bring her into our bedroom before she stopped, but when I woke up this morning she was curled up at the bottom of our bed and sleeping peacefully," she says.

I laugh. "Next time I'll bring her down with me."

"Brilliant idea," she agrees.

"All right then. Speak to you soon."

"Oh, wait a minute. Irina wants to say hello."

Irina comes on the phone and babbles something to me and I babble right back to her. As I put the phone down I feel my heart swell with all the love I am surrounded by.

I pull a throw from one of the armchairs and drape it around my body as I walk back to the bedroom. I stop at the doorway. Jack is lying naked on the bedcovers. His dick is so hard it is at right angles to his body. He raises his eyebrows.

"What?" I ask coyly.

"What's with the blanket?" he asks, and there is that look in his eyes again.

I shrug.

"Don't you want me to see your pussy?"

My heart starts racing with excitement. I nod.

"In that case …" He crooks his finger and I walk towards him and stand by the side of the bed. Reaching under the throw, he slides his hand up my thigh. "Open," he commands.

I spread my legs and he slips a finger into me. I moan. He moves it in and out of me, as if testing for slickness.

"Are you going to fight me about the blanket?" he asks softly.

I shake my head.

"Good. Lose it."

I grasp a handful of material and pull it off my body.

He growls with satisfaction, his eyes greedily watching his finger plunging in and out of me. He takes his finger out, feeds it into his mouth and sucks it while pre-cum leaks from him. I bend my head and lick his thick cream. Like for like. He smiles.

"Get on your back and open up for me," he says.

I do as he asks. Grabbing his cock, he rubs the massive tip in my wetness before thrusting in. I cry out at the sudden intrusion.

"Fuck, you're so tight," he snarls.

Holding still inside me to allow me to adjust to his size, he lowers his face and sweeps his tongue inside my mouth. My hips jerk upwards to accommodate more of him and he begins to rut away. The headboard smacks the wall with each hard slam and I groan loudly at each pass.

"You like me to cum in your sweet cunt, Princess?'

I moan and his hips thrust faster.

The bed rocks like a boat in the ocean. Small, weird, animal-like cries come out of my mouth, but I can't stop them and I don't care to. I'm about to have my fifth climax. My thighs clench his cock as my body arches off the bed. The tip of the iceberg breaks and the whole damn thing crumbles into the sea in one giant show of fierce heat and pure ecstasy.

He thrusts as hard as he can and climaxes deep inside, filling me with his warm seed.

Twenty-seven

Jack

I'm too old to be so fucking insane for a girl, but I can't bear the thought of letting her go. I feel as horny as fuck, even though I've just fucked her in the shower. I want her to stay in my bed this night and every night from now on, but she tells me she needs to go back.

Her puppy misses her!

Fucking hell, *I* miss her.

Anyway, we agree that she'll go back and get her dog and the three of us will spend the weekend together. But I hate the thought of her going back to Cheshire. I mean, any random man could be looking at her, touching her. A red haze fills my brain at the thought of another man touching her.

Fuck, see what I mean by going insane for a chick.

I've got an eleven o'clock appointment that I've already missed and my secretary/receptionist is droning on in my ear about it.

"Yeah, yeah, I'll be there in time for the 11.30," I tell her.

I let her chew my ear off for a bit more. She deserves it for putting up with some of our patients, and she's probably taken a bit of shit for my missed morning appointments. Besides I'm in an excellent mood this morning.

"I'm thinking of giving you a raise," I say.

She stops mid-sentence. "How much?"

I laugh. She's Irish all right. "We'll talk about it when I get there."

"I'll be sitting right here waiting," she comes back crisply.

I ring off still smiling.

"You seem to be on *really* good terms with your secretary," Sofia comments.

"Yeah, we get on."

"Oh, so how old is she?"

Is she fucking jealous? The idea is intriguing. "Hmmm ... not sure," I say softly, "but she looks good for her age."

Her eyes widen, and I see the flash of jealously that she can't hide. It makes my cock jerk. I hate (as in I'd rather be boiled alive) jealous women fucking clinging on and checking up on me, but right now I can't get enough of her jealousy. I want to see her hurt for me.

Her eyes dull and she quickly drops her face, her beautiful hair sliding forward to cover her cheeks, and instantly I feel bad for teasing her. Just knowing she can hurt for me is enough. I never want to cause her even a moment of hurt. She's suffered enough in her short life.

I pull her towards me and her body molds to mine. I put a finger under her chin and lift it up. "Karen's happily married and she's not my type, anyway," I tell her.

The sparkle comes back to her eyes. "Oh yeah?"

I kiss her cute nose. "Yeah."

"What's your type then?" she asks, licking her bottom lip. Heavens above, my girl is flirting with me.

I grind her hips so she can feel my rigid cock. "I'm looking at her."

"I never dreamed it could be like this," she whispers.

"Neither did I," I confess.

She looks up at me with her mouth slightly parted, and God knows what it is about this woman, but I have to fight not to throw her on the floor and fuck her right there, or better still take her against the wall. Standing sex. We haven't done that yet. So many things we haven't done. But I got my stupid 11.30 appointment with another pointless celebrity waiting for me.

Then she bites her bottom lip. The little minx did that purposely.

"Stop doing that," I growl.

Her eyes go big. "What this?" she says, and bites it again.

Oh, fuck. I'm in so much trouble. All I want to do is stuff my cock into her lush mouth. Fuck my 11.30. I'll reschedule and work through my lunch hour on Monday, or something. Anything.

I grip my Princess's hips tighter and push her body away from mine.

"What are you doing?" she asks innocently, but her eyes are glazed, the pupils massive. She's so turned on I can smell her pussy. The scent is actually driving me crazy.

"It's your fault I've got an erection. So get on your knees and suck me off," I tell her as I unbuckle my belt and take my cock out of my boxers.

With a secretive little smile she gets on her knees and looks up at me through her eyelashes. Very, very flirtatious and very, very, very sexy.

"Open up, Princess," I say holding my cock.

She opens her mouth and I feed my cock into her sweet mouth. With a groan I rake my fingers through her long, silky hair. She sucks me softly, closing her eyes, and moaning with the taste of my cock. It's so hot to see a woman enjoy sucking me off so much that I almost climax right then and there. I clench my hands in her hair. I don't want it to be over yet.

Slowly but surely she sucks me to the back of her throat until every inch is inside her. I look down at her, and I swear it's the prettiest thing I've ever seen. My cock completely buried in her face. She does this little thing with her tongue that feels as if she's milking my dick for cum. More cum leaks out of me and gets swallowed by her.

Oh fuck. No one has given me head like this before. I want it to last forever, but it's so good I can't last much longer. I throw my head back and feel the thick veins in my shaft pulsing and throbbing, ready to shoot my load. I try to stop myself from climaxing, and a massive shiver goes through my body.

Realizing I'm going to nut, she starts sucking harder and deeper.

"I want you to drink down my cum so that when I leave here I know you've got my cum in your belly," I growl, gripping her hair and pulling her towards my groin.

I shoot my load and her throat closes over my dick as she swallows every last drop. The only thing on my mind is the craving to push her on the floor and eat her pussy, but she is on her feet in a flash and tucking my cock back into my underpants.

"You don't want to miss your 11.30," she whispers.

I devour her lips and mouth, and then I run out of that apartment as if the devil is snapping at my heels, because all I want to do is drag her back to bed, and fuck her sweet pussy again and again.

Twenty-eight

Sofia

As I leave the castle with Mika's warm body tucked under my arm, Lena gently warns me not to fall in love too quickly. Because I have never known kindness from a man she believes I might be susceptible to falling hard at the first act of kindness. I don't tell her she is too late. I have already succumbed. Hard and big.

I can't fully describe my magical weekend with Jack and Mika. After all the pain I had been through I can't believe I can be so lucky. It is just perfect. I've never known such happiness. I arrive at Jack's place in the afternoon. His apartment looks unlived in. It's very modern and kind of cold actually. The kitchen is completely brand new. It looks like it has never been used. There is not a scratch on all the highly polished surfaces. I open his fridge, and there is nothing in it but an out-of-date carton of milk, a six pack of beer, and a slab of butter.

We go shopping at the little corner shop. A sweet Polish woman serves us. We buy milk, eggs, bacon, bread, strawberry jam, cereal, popcorn and ice cream from her.

That night we order pizza and the three of us of make pigs of ourselves. I eat so much I can hardly move. When Jack carries me to his bed and buries his face between my legs, Mika sits on her bed and watches until she is certain that the animal sounds I am making are not distress calls. Then she lays her head down and closes her eyes contentedly.

Every time Jack wakes me up to rut, she raises her head curiously, but she never tries to come on the bed. In the morning I offer to make breakfast, but Jack says he'd rather I save my energy for fucking, and off he heads into the kitchen.

He comes back with two plates of burnt eggs. I laugh and we eat cereals and popcorn and ice cream in bed instead. Well, what can I say? Ice cream, bed, and Jack. Dirty sheets. Wicked combination.

In the shower, the water bounces off his eyelashes and nose as he pours body shampoo into the palm of his hand. I watch him rub his palms and cup my breasts. The water, the silk of the soap suds, his hot hands. It all makes me quite dizzy. He washes my hair, his hands hypnotic and sensuous. He sucks my skin and leaves little hickeys all over my body.

"I like seeing them," he says.

"Why?" I ask.

He takes a nipple in his mouth and sucks it for some time. "Men are like dogs. They like to mark their territory."

"Am I your territory?"

"Like you wouldn't believe."

Afterwards, we take Mika to the park. While we walk I have to try not to think about his hard body walking next to me and how quickly his cock will respond if I just brush my hand against him.

A woman with a pitbull walks by us and Mika stops to smell him. I am terrified, but it is Mika who gets aggressive. She jumps on his back, then growls at him. The woman just laughs. She thinks it's cute. But I know her dog can break Mika's neck in half. Horrified, I snatch Mika up and hold her close to my body.

"Stupid Mika," I scold. "Don't do that again."

Mika whines and shows me her sad eyes. I can never stay angry. I pepper her head with kisses. "I'm sorry I shouted at you," I croon into her warm silky-soft ear.

"You really love her, don't you?" Jack notes quietly.

"Yes, she is my daughter."

He nods and we carry on walking.

We stop at a pancake café and sit at one of the small, rickety tables outside. I know my nose must be red with cold, but he looks at it as if it is the most beautiful thing he has ever seen. When he looks at me like that I feel as if I have been transported into a movie or another realm. The waitress comes and Jack orders half the menu. She raises her eyebrows. "One pancake is usually sufficient for one person," she reminds.

I laugh. "Are we going to eat all that?"

"Of course not. But this moment feels like a dream. And dreams should be abundant."

I know exactly what he means. That is what I have been feeling too. As if I am in a dream. At any moment I could wake up.

Our order arrives. Plates upon plates of steaming pancakes. The waitress drags another table over and joins it to ours. I stare at all the food. It seems a shame to waste it, but I couldn't give up this moment. The cold, Jack, Mika, the people passing us as if we don't exist. I have never been in such a situation. It is perfect.

Jack has the breakfast pancake with eggs and bacon, and I try the one with figs and honey and walnuts. I pour syrup over it all, cut a piece and put it in my mouth. It's absolutely delicious. Part of the dream I am dreaming.

"Let's try a bit of everything," I say.

"Whatever you want, baby."

I reach for the blueberry cream pancake, tear a corner, slip it into my mouth and chew it.

He stares at me in silence. As if watching me eat is the most wondrous thing ever.

"Stop staring," I say, embarrassed.

He runs his finger on the inside of my wrist. "I could watch you eat all day, Princess."

"Why do you call me Princess?"

"You live in a castle, don't you?"

I nod.

"The only fairytale I remember reading is Beauty and the Beast. That's me and you, babe."

I giggle. "You're no beast."

"Let anybody try taking you away from me." There is no accompanying smile in his face. He is dead serious.

"Nobody else wants me," I murmur.

He scowls. "There better fucking not be."

I laugh and eat until my jeans feel tight. "I can't move," I say, rubbing my belly.

"Want me to carry you home?"

I laugh. I've never been so happy in my life. "I'm going to get so fat," I complain.

"Good," he says heartily. "I like a bit of meat on my woman."

My woman. I like the sound of that.

It starts drizzling. The waitress comes out waving her hands frantically. There is something wrong with the mechanism that controls the awning so she wants to move all our food and us inside.

"No," I say.

She looks at me as if I am mad. "The food will get wet."

"Bring us the bill," Jack tells her.

We settle the bill. Jack puts Mika into his jacket and we walk in the rain back to his home. When we get in we tear at each other's clothes. As if three hours without each other's body is too long. We have sex on the floor. I open my body to him, to each hard thrust, and the semen when it comes. I welcome it as it spurts thick and deep into my waiting body.

Jack picks me off the floor. "Come on, Princess. Let's do it properly on the bed."

Twenty-nine

Sofia

I'm lying on a hospital bed in my private room waiting to be prepped for my surgery when Jack walks in. I stare at him. It is a strange thing to see him in his scrubs. I never thought it possible, but he looks even more handsome than he normally does. Butterflies flutter about in my stomach.

"Are you nervous?" I ask him.

He grins confidently. "No. Are you?"

"No. I trust you implicitly."

"Good. Can I have a taste?"

My eyes widen. "What?"

"One last taste before they wheel you in."

I shake my head at his brazenness. "That's not very professional, is it?"

"Nope. And that's the way it'll be forever between us."

He locks the door and walks over to me, mischief in his eyes. He lifts the white gown. "Go on. Be a dirty girl, for me."

I hesitate only for a second. What the hell. I want it as much as he does. I spread my legs and he swipes his tongue along my seam. Then he eats my pussy, the way only Jack Irish knows how until all the stars collide and I shatter on his tongue.

"I've left a wet spot on the bed now. The nurses will see it," I say.

"Don't worry about it, Princess. They're used to all kinds of bodily fluids on the bed."

I chew my lip. Something's been worrying me. Maybe I won't wake up from the anesthetic. Maybe this will be my last time with him. I catch his hand. I want to tell him I love him. He should know. He looks at me expectantly, but the words that come out of my mouth

are totally different. "Do you think you'll get bored of eating me one day?"

"I don't bore easily. I've been drinking milk since I was a baby and I still love it," he says with a wink.

I smile nervously. I really want to tell him I love him. Just in case I don't wake up, but before I can pick up the courage, there is a knock on the door.

Jack opens the door and a nurse bustles in.

"Oh, doctor," she says in a flustered voice.

He smiles cheekily at her. "Good morning, Nurse."

He kisses me on the head. "I'll be back to see you before they take you down to the anesthetist."

While the nurse is taking my blood pressure, Lena comes in. I smile broadly at her. She has never been the same since the afternoon I showed her my back. She howled when she saw it, and the pitiful sound reminded me of our mother. The way she wailed when she lost her baby. That is the only time she wept like that, but it's never left my mind. She never even cried like that when my father broke her limbs, or that time he plunged her hand in boiling water.

I held Lena, but I couldn't stop her from crying. I learned that day that no matter how strong she seems we are both irreparably damaged, and all it requires is a trigger to expose that incurable wound. There was nothing I could say or do that would comfort her. When she began to call out to our dead brother, I became frightened. I called Guy. He had gone to Manchester for a meeting. He dropped everything and flew back immediately. Only when she was in his arms did she quieten down. Ever since that day she has become even more protective over me.

"Are you ready?" she asks with a gentle smile.

I grin back. "Yes."

She walks up to the bed. "Good. It'll go well. Jack's one of the best."

At that moment I get emotional and my eyes flood with tears. She entwines her fingers with mine and switches to Russian. "Oh, darling. Don't cry. You'll be fine. I'll be waiting right here for you."

I swallow hard and nod.

She takes a tissue out of her purse and dries my eyes. "I'm so proud of you. You've come so far. You're the bravest person I know."

"I'm not brave. I couldn't have done any of it without you and Guy."

She shakes her head. "We gave you the knife. You cut the ropes all by yourself. Every single one. You are free now. Fly the way you were always meant to."

I grasp her hand and kiss it.

"You should be leaving now, Ma'am," the nurse says.

Lena lays both her hands on my cheeks and kisses me gently on the

forehead. "I'll be waiting outside. All will be well."

I watch her leave. A male nurse comes in and starts wheeling me down the corridor. At a station full of equipment Jack appears. He already has his face mask on and his eyes sparkle like the bluest, brightest stones.

"Just relax, Princess," he says.

A mask is put over my face and the anesthetist asks me to count backwards. I don't count, I stare into Jack's eyes and tell him with my eyes that I love him ... until blackness comes.

When I wake up, my mouth is dry and I am lying on my front with my cheek resting on the pillow. The first thing my searching eyes see is Jack sitting on a chair nearby, but he is not looking at me. He is staring out of the window into the night, his expression far away. For a few seconds I stare at him in shock. This is surely not the face of a happy man. I thought he was happy with me. Then as if he feels my scrutiny he turns towards me and his face changes instantly. He smiles.

"Hey," he whispers.

I watch him get up and come to me. "Your surgery went well and I think you'll be really happy with the result."

He sounds like a doctor talking to his patient. Then he strokes my hair and he becomes my Jack again. I ask for water. He gives it to me and watches me intently while I drink it.

Though I smile and answer all his questions about how I feel, that faraway, unhappy expression I saw on his face when he thought no one was looking remains at the back of my mind, fraying the edges of my happiness.

Thirty

Jack

As a patient walks out of my consulting room, Karen buzzes me to say that Lena is at Reception waiting to see me.

"Send her in," I tell her, rubbing the back of my neck. I shouldn't be here, but I've had to work through my backlog. The people I've messed around because I can't get to work in time in the mornings anymore.

Lena comes to sit in front of me. She puts her purse on my table and smiles at me.

I lean back in my chair and look at her curiously. "What's up, Lena?"

"First of all I want to thank you for what you did for Sofia. I'm so grateful to you."

That's not why she's really here. "You don't have to thank me, Lena. Anybody in my shoes would have done the same."

She shifts in her chair. "I don't just mean the surgery. You've made her happy."

I nod. I know I've made Sofia happy, but she's made me happy too. Very happy. "The emotion is mutual," I say softly.

She smiles again. "You know how you and Sofia agreed that for the next week she's going to stay at your place and you were going to take care of her?"

I watch her without expression. "Yeah?"

"You still have to work during the daytime, right?"

"Uh ... huh."

"Who will watch her then?"

"I'm taking tomorrow off to be with her, but once her bandages are removed she will be able to move around and do almost everything for herself. Besides,

I'll only be thirty minutes away. If she needs anything at all she only has to call me."

She clears her throat. "Here is what I was thinking. I was thinking that you should move into our apartment for the next couple of weeks. This way I can stay with her during the day, and when you come back I can go back to Cheshire and you can take over her care."

I stare at her, surprised. I have to admit, never in my life, have I come across such dedication and love between two sisters. One part of me resents having to share even an ounce of Sofia, and another can't help but be in awe of such a rare and beautiful phenomenon.

"There's no need for that. You're welcome to come and stay with her at my place during the day," I offer.

"I have my baby and all her things are at the apartment, but I will come to yours if you'd rather not stay in our place. You can both move into our room since it is much bigger and has an ensuite. It'll be good for you too. Going to work will be more convenient. You'll shave ten minutes off your travelling time," she says persuasively.

I rub my chin reflectively. "What does your husband think of this ... arrangement?"

She smiles. "Actually, it was his idea. I was obsessing about how to sort out the problem last night, and he suggested it."

My eyebrows rise. The last time Guy and I met he wasn't too impressed with me. In fact, I distinctively remember he was sipping hard on the haterade.

"So, are you okay with the idea?" she asks.

I shrug. "Sure. I could move in for a week."

She exhales with relief. "Thank you, Jack. I am so glad. In ordinary circumstances I would have preferred to have taken her back to Cheshire with me, but since I honestly believe that she

will heal faster with you, I'm happy to
come down every day and care for her."

I spend the first night in the
hospital with Sofia. After she falls asleep
I go down the corridor, get myself a
lousy coffee from the vending machine,
and sit down on one of the couches. It is
late and there is no one around. It's an
odd feeling to be in the hospital at this
time. I look out of the glass door and see
people walking past.

The nurse who had come to prep
Sofia passes the front desk, sees me, and
walks towards me.

"That was a nasty thing on her back.
What bastard did that to her?" she asks.

"I don't know," I say.

"I'd kill him if I saw him," she
mutters angrily. "It's just not right that
he should be walking about alive and
well. The idea that a man could do that

to a woman and walk about free makes me so angry," she says.

I say nothing. I can't. I'm holding it all back by the skin of my teeth. She has no idea how I feel about that monster. I wouldn't just kill him. I'd flay him alive and make him suffer for days.

"Anyway, that's me done for the night. I've got my daughter flying in from Germany so we're going out." She looks happy.

"Have a great time," I say.

She moves away and I stare into my coffee. It's Africa all over again. There was not a thing I could do about anything there either. In the end shit happened and I was hired to put a plaster over their rotting cancers. I feel like going out getting totally plastered and smashing something. That always helped in the past, but I know it won't help tonight. Nothing will help.

I lift my head and look out of the glass walls. The sky is velvety and full of stars. If there is a God out there, then let that sadistic beast find his retribution.

Deliberately I pick up my coffee and drink it, trash the cup, and go back to Sofia's room.

I open the door and find her awake.

"I thought you'd gone home," she says.

"Not without you, Princess. I ain't going nowhere without you."

Thirty-one

Sofia

The technique Jack used is called a scar revision with geometric line closure. I have been prescribed painkillers, but I think I am too happy to feel any real pain so I don't take them.

Forty-eight hours after my operation Jack takes the bandages off in his bathroom.

"Hmmm …" he says.

"What does it look like?" I ask anxiously.

Jack positions me in front of the bathroom mirror. "Close your eyes."

With bated breath I follow his instruction.

"Go on and open your eyes now."

I obey, and Jack is holding another mirror behind me. I look into it and inhale sharply. Even though my wounds are still very swollen and raw the ugliness is gone! All the thickened and tethered scars, the snarled skin, and the angry red and brown valleys have been taken away. All that is left is the unharmed skin. I cover my mouth with my hands and meet his gaze in the mirror.

"Like it?" he asks.

I spin around, and cupping his face between my palms, kiss him. For a long time I simply lose myself in our kiss, the evergreen sensation of his lips, the taste of him, the smell of him, the feel of my man. Then I pull my face away.

"It looks ... amazing," I whisper into his mouth.

He holds me a few inches away from him. "It's not finished yet. This is only the beginning. In two weeks you will start wearing silicone sheets. Then, when all your incisions are well healed in about four weeks, I will increase the volume of whatever few depressions are left with fat transfers under the tissue.

After that I'll resurface the remaining scars with a series of Fraxel laser restructuring."

I smile at him.

"Just when you don't think it can't get any better you will have microdermabrasion treatment. After that the scars will be so fine you'll have to look really hard to see them."

I look up at him in awe. He is my savior, my protector, my all.

He shakes his head. "How can you look so sweet after everything you have been through? It's simply incredible that you are so untouched by the evil and cruelty you have been forced to live with," he marvels.

I look deep into his beautiful eyes. "Thank you."

"Thank me properly," he whispers back.

My breathing catches. "How?"

He hooks his fingers into my panties and pulls them down my thighs. They pool around my feet. He grabs my ass and lifts me up. I curl my legs around his waist, pressing my wet heat into his abdomen. There is nothing separating us except his thin shirt. I lift it up. Now there is just my open naked sex rubbing slowly and deliberately on his skin. It's like I'm leaving my scent on him. Marking him as mine.

His eyes darken with crazy need as he carries me to the countertop next to the sink and sets me down.

"Open up, my beauty," he orders, his voice husky.

I open my legs wide. Gazing into my eyes he slips two fingers into me and curling them expertly stokes my inner walls. I whimper as he kneels between my thighs. I feel his hot breath on my open pussy before his mouth clamps down on my clit and he starts sucking greedily. Always as if he is starving. As if he can never get enough.

I look down and his other hand is working between his own legs, his movements rough and frenzied. One of his favorite things is tasting me as he jerks off. I've never had a man who loved my taste so much. I open my legs even wider to give him more access, and he immediately growls with lust and satisfaction.

Our eyes lock.

The orgasm hits me hard and fast.

One moment I'm nearly there and waiting to ride the wave, and the next, my eyes are rolling to the back of my head. I'm screaming like a banshee and gushing all over his hand, his mouth, and his chin. I still find it embarrassing and dirty that he drinks my juices, but it is also indescribably sexy.

With his fingers still buried inside me he stands. Pulling his fingers out he feeds all eight inches of his big, hot, girth into me, filling me to the brim. My head drops back and I moan with pleasure.

"This. Is. How. You. Thank. Me," he grunts as he thrusts in and out of my clenched muscles.

"Harder," I pant with every hard slam.

He shuts me up by crashing his mouth against mine, pushing his tongue into it and making me suck it. The gesture is at once aggressive, dominating and completely possessive. As he picks up speed his mouth separates from mine.

"Tell me you're mine," he says.

"I'm yours," I reply.

With a hoarse sound, he spills his hot seed inside me.

"Sometimes I can't believe you're real," I tell him.

"I have the same damn problem," he mutters.

Smiling, I lean forward and lie on his chest. His big arms come around my waist and his cock twitches deliciously inside me.

Thirty-two

Sofia

That Thursday Lena takes my class for me. When I ask her how it went she says that Lori came, but when she saw her, she immediately turned around and ran out of the room. Lena also says that she looked frightened and pale.

I wonder what is wrong, but there is absolutely nothing I can do except wait for my next class and hope she will attend. In the meantime, my life is a big bowl of the reddest, ripest, sweetest cherries. It is food, laughter, fun, and sex. Oh, my God, the sex.

Even though I am still lightly bandaged it never stops Jack. The only position we don't attempt is with me on my back, otherwise, there is no limit to his creativity. I find myself sitting up with my legs open very often. On beds, tables, chairs, at the end of the bath. Oh, and sometimes he'll make me stand and hook a leg over his shoulder while he helps himself. Like I said, we are limited only by his creativity.

Usually, Lena will arrive by ten and stay until he comes back home. We talk, we read, we play with Irina, we go for short walks. The time passes quickly and Thursday comes around. I persuade Jack and Lena that I feel well enough to take my music class, but it's not the class I care about. Its Lori.

I feel as if I must see her. After all the years I spent living off my wits, my instinct has been honed and is very strong. I know that something is wrong. I feel it in my bones. We go to the center and I wait for her in my classroom. The other girls arrive on time, but Lori does not. Disappointed, I start the class without her. We are almost finished when she bursts though the door. She is breathing hard and her eyes are wild with terror.

"What is it?" I ask standing up from the piano stool.

She rushes up to me and says urgently, "Please help me, Sofia. My mother is very ill. I'm afraid she might be dying."

I take her hand. "Take me to her." She starts pulling me to the door. I know I am not supposed to run and I can feel the strain on my wounds, but it can't be helped. I know this is an emergency. We run down the corridor and open the door that leads to the reception. Jack and Lena are waiting for me there.

"Whoa, whoa, whoa," Jack cautions. He opens his hands in a gesture that is meant to convey what the fuck are you doing.

"Lori's mother is very ill. We have to help her," I tell them.

He holds his hands up. "Just calm down everybody." He looks at Lori. "What's going on?"

"Mama has been ill for two weeks, but now she's really bad."

"Don't worry, Lori. We'll help your mother." He looks up at me. "I'll go. You stay here with your sister."

Immediately I feel Lori squeeze my hand. I look down at her and she is begging me with her eyes to go with her.

I look at Jack. "I want to come."

"You don't need to."

"Please," I beg.

"All right," he says. "But no running."

"Let Robert drive you. This way if you need to take her mother to hospital, Robert can help move her, and he can just drop you off at the entrance of A&E. You don't have to park."

"Good thinking, Lena. Thanks," Jack says.

We walk quickly to the car and drive to her house. She lives in one of the four high rise apartments behind Kids Rule. As we walk towards the graffiti sprayed entrance, we see Andrew, one of the boys who comes to the center, standing by the heavy door. He smiles at us, but looks embarrassed.

I wonder why until I notice the older boys standing beside him. I can tell straight away they are small time drug dealers. I'd know those shifty eyes and stance from a mile away. For years I saw them hanging around the brothels.

It makes me sad to think of Andrew hanging around with that crowd, because it's only a matter of time before he becomes one of them. I like Andrew. He's an intelligent and sweet boy. I see that Jack has noticed too, because he is scowling as he hits the elevator button.

"Is your house in this block too?' Jack asks as we wait for the elevator.

"Number sixty-four," he calls as the elevator doors open.

Jack nods and we hurry inside. Inside it smells of piss. We get off at the fourth floor. Lori leads the way to a green door down the corridor. She puts her key in and opens it. The stench that comes out is vomit inducing.

"This way," she says, and we are led to a cold bedroom with the curtains pulled shut. A pale woman is under the covers.

"Mama. I've brought some people to help you." Lori sobs.

Her mother is so weak she is barely able to open her eyes. She breathes with difficulty. "Lori," she groans feebly, then begins speaking to her in a foreign language.

"Mama, they're not going to tell Papa. I know them. They're good people," Lori says.

Jack moves forward. "Can your mother speak English?" he asks Lori.

"A little bit."

"Tell me her symptoms. What's wrong with her?"

"She has a fever and a stomach ache and she is tired all the time. And she cannot eat."

"For how long?"

"Two weeks, but she is getting worse."

Jack moves the bedclothes. Instead of trying to unzip her he pulls her dress up over her legs to expose her stomach. He touches her lower abdomen close to her belly button and she groans. He touches another area to the right and she screams in agony.

He looks up at Lori. "Lori, go and call the elevator. Then ask Robert to bring the car as close to the front door as possible."

"What's wrong with Mama?" she asks in a small, frightened voice.

"We don't have time to talk now. Hurry up and do what I asked you to. We can talk later."

With a sob Lori turns around and runs out of the room.

He wraps Lori's mother up in the blankets and slips his arms under her head and her knees.

"Leave the front door wedged open and go and hold the elevator doors open for me, Sofia," he says, heaving her up.

I quickly do his bidding. The elevator comes quickly so I have to keep on jamming it open. He kicks away the chair I left to keep the doors open and walks towards me.

Lori's mother is mumbling incoherently.

I get in and press the ground floor button.

"What's wrong with her?" I ask once we're inside the lift.

"I think she has a ruptured appendix."

I stare at him in shock. I have heard of people who die from burst appendixes. The doors groan open and I walk on ahead and hold the entrance door open. Andrew is still hanging around and comes running up to us.

"Want some help, Jack?" he asks.

"Thanks, Andrew. I got this one."

Carefully, Jack lays the woman in the backseat. Then he asks Robert to get out of the car and instructs Lori to hold her mother's head and comfort her because it will be a difficult journey for her. Then he tells me to get into the front passenger seat.

He slides into the driver's seat and starts the car.

Thirty-three

Sofia

"**W**hat's wrong with my mother?" Lori asks in a frightened little voice.

"It looks like your mother's appendix might have ruptured, but the good news is I think we got to her in time. She just needs to have it removed so that she will feel better."

As Jack had predicted, the journey was very difficult for Lori's mother. The vibration of the car causes her to grimace, and every tiny bump makes her cry out in agony. There is not a thing I can do.

Once at the hospital, Lori's mother is immediately wheeled away. While Lori and I are in the Waiting Room, Jack goes off to see what help he can give. He comes back to tell us that she has to have emergency surgery.

Later he pulls me aside and tells me that her burst appendix went gangrenous. "The appendix and all evidence of gangrene were removed, and the area irrigated and inspected. Luckily, scans indicate no other organs, especially her intestines, were effected. She will be on heavy administration of antibiotics to help clear the infection."

"Will she make it?" I whisper, horrified.

He nods. "I think so."

Lori's mother is in the theater for ages. Finally, she is wheeled out. The operation is a success, but she will have to stay at the hospital for some time.

That night Lori stays with us. I put her in the nanny's room. When I go to tuck her into bed she looks at me sadly.

"She will be all right, won't she?"

"Yes. The worst is over now. In a few weeks she should be ready to come home."

She looks worried. "A few weeks?"

"I'm afraid so, sweetie."

"After tonight I could go back and stay at my house, couldn't I?"

I stare at her. "What? Alone?"

She nods bravely.

"What about your dad? Wouldn't you like to stay with him?"

She shrinks from me. Fear flashes into her eyes. "You won't tell my father will you?"

"No, no, not if you don't want us to," I assure her hurriedly.

She shakes her head. "You mustn't. Please."

"Okay. I won't."

She nods.

"Are you and your mother running away from him?" I ask softly.

"Yes. He used to beat us. We ran away from Romania. We've been hiding here for the last year, but he went to my

 278

Nan's house and said he knew we are in England and that he would find us."

"Is that why you don't talk to anybody?"

"Yes. Mama says the more people who know where we are the easier it will be for him to find us."

"You and your mother are very brave," I tell her.

"My mother is," she says simply. I think of my own mother. If only she had had the courage to do what Lori's mother had done. Run away with all of us. How different life would have been for all of us. But that is the past and cannot be changed.

"Shouldn't we tell your grandmother? Wouldn't she want to know?"

"Yes, we should tell her."

"Do you know how to contact her?"

"I have her phone number."

"Good. We can call her tomorrow."

"Okay."

"Does she live alone?"

"Yes."

"I see. Perhaps we can invite her to come over."

"She won't be able to afford it," she says sadly.

"I will pay for her. She will come as my guest. You can stay with us until she comes. Then if you want, you can even go up to the castle and stay the night in the tower with your grandmother. Would you like that?"

Her eyes light up. "Really?"

"Tomorrow we'll send someone to clean your house so that when your grandmother comes it will be sparkling clean."

She looks shamefaced. "I did try to clean it."

"Hey, you did amazing."

"Thank you, Sofia."

"Oh, little sweetheart. I did nothing. Like you I wouldn't have known what to do. It was all Jack."

She shakes her head, making her hair tumble about on the pillow. "No, it

was you. I would not have been brave enough to go to anyone else."

"Well, thankfully, it's all in the past. How about we say that Jack, you and me together saved the day?"

She nods.

I smile at her. "Now, time to close these cute little eyes and go to sleep now, don't you think?"

"Can Mika stay with me tonight?"

I touch her little button nose. "Of course she can."

"Thank you."

"Up ,Mika," I say, and she immediately jumps on the bed.

"Stay and guard little Lori tonight, okay," I say stroking her silky head. She licks my hand and I kiss the top of her head.

"Goodnight both of you," I say, leaving the door slightly ajar.

I walk down the corridor and into my bedroom. Jack is going through the messages on his phone. I close the door and lean against it.

He puts his phone down and smiles. "Everything okay?"

I nod.

"Lock that door and come here," he says.

'We'll have to be very quiet tonight," I tell him.

"Fuck being quiet," he says, picking something up from the bed and letting it swing from his pointer finger."

I giggle. "You bought a gag?"

"Chance favors the prepared mind."

Thirty-four

Jack

https://www.youtube.com/watch?v=PNc278W45ck

One day after Lori and her grandmother return from Sofia's tower at the castle and return to her mother's apartment, I get home from work and find Guy in the living room. He walks up to me, puts one hand on my shoulder, grabs my other hand and shakes it firmly.

"I was wrong about you. No matter what happens in the future, you've done more for Sofia than I would have thought possible. She's a new person," he says sincerely.

I shrug casually, but I can't help the glow of pride I feel inside. I know I have been good for her.

"No, really," he insists. "Every day I see her blossom and become more and more radiant. Sometimes I look at her and she doesn't even seem to be the same person anymore."

I smile, and don't tell him about my deepest concern. Yes, her body is repaired, but that may be just one battle won. The war is far from over. The real problem is Sofia and I have sex, we laugh, we eat, we dance, but we never talk about her past. Nothing. Even when I have tried to tell her about mine, she leans forward and listens eagerly, absorbing every little detail greedily, then instead of offering even the smallest tit bit about herself, she'll say something like, "Guess what I'm wearing underneath this dress," or "God, I'd love to have you inside me now."

That's like waving a red rag at a bull. Action guaranteed. We'll have sex and the moment will pass. Of course, I don't want to hear about all those men. Even the thought is enough to make me feel sick to my stomach and want to kill someone, but I don't want her whole past to be a no-go area.

I know she is keenly aware of how possessive and jealous I am, but how would it hurt to throw a little scrap about her childhood in my direction. I know her father was a cruel and sadistic man, but we can't go through our lives never referring to him.

Sometimes I'm even tempted to ask Lena to tell me what really happened. Just so I understand. Just so I have a picture of her as a child. I want to understand. I know I own her body, but that is not enough. I want it all. Mind, body and soul.

"Have a drink with me?" Guy offers.

"Sure. I'll have a beer."

He takes a bottle out of the mini fridge under the bar for me and pours himself a whiskey.

"Glass?" he asks.

"Nah."

He brings my bottle to me. I smile my thanks and take a swig. "So where are the girls?"

"Lena is helping Sofia dress."

I frown. "Why?'

"It's kind of a surprise."

I look at him warily. "Right."

"Here they are now."

Lena comes in first and she is grinning like a Cheshire cat. Then Sofia comes in and it is like a punch in the gut. My eyes widen and my jaw actually drops. Jesus! She is wearing a red dress made from some kind of slinky material. And she is wearing high heels. And her hair has been styled in waves that flow down her back. She is fucking stunning.

"Hi," she says softly.

"Wow! Just wow," I reply. My voice sounds gruff. She has never dressed up for me before.

She blushes and looks even more beautiful.

"Well, we'll be off then," Lena says.

"Bye," I say, and I don't even turn my head to watch them leave.

The front door shuts and suddenly the apartment is too quiet.

I walk up to her, take her hand and twirl her around slowly. "How can a woman be so beautiful," I whisper.

"I'm not beautiful. My sister is the beauty in our fami-."

I place my finger on her lips. "Don't. Don't spit in our good fortune. We are the luckiest people on earth."

A smile trembles on her lips.

"Where are we going?" I ask, lifting my finger away from her lips.

"We are going to a classical concert."

I groan. "Don't tell me you're taking me to a place where I have to sit in the dark next to you with a hard on for an hour."

She giggles.

My goodness. How beautiful is my girl.

"You'll survive. I wanted to treat you with my first bit of money. It's the rent from my apartment. Guy and Lena gave it to me so I'd have my own money."

"In that case, I am honored."

She takes me to see Vanessa Mae, and I have to admit the woman was amazing. She looks good and is as buzzed and energetic as any rock star, and played the violin like an electric dream.

Afterwards, we go for a meal in a fancy restaurant. We have our first argument when the bill comes. I'm glad she has her own money and that it makes her feel happy, but I'm damned if my woman is going to pay the restaurant bill. We end our disagreement in the car park with my tongue in her mouth.

I'll never forget the strip show she put on until my dying day.

Thirty-five

Sofia

https://www.youtube.com/watch?v=eJS ik6ejkro
(Running)

I move into Jack's apartment ten days after my surgery. Every day I stand in front of the mirror and turn around to look at my back. Every day I see it improving. The redness is going. The swelling will take six months to completely go away but it is slowly coming down.

Sometimes I'll leave my hair down and walk around naked. I could never do that before because my hair would get stuck in the uneven bits of flesh and irritate me, reminding me of my scar.

This is without doubt the happiest time of my life. One day we attend the wedding of an acquaintance of Jack, Noah Abramovich, to his startlingly beautiful bride.

"We're just going to show our faces, then disappear," Jack tells me, but when we get there we are treated as honored guests and invited to sit at the very front. The famous pianist Alexander Malenkov is there. I nearly die when he comes forward to shake my hand. I'm so flustered by the encounter Jack gets jealous.

"Do I need to go punch his lights out?" he growls.

I laugh. "I don't fancy him. I just think he's incredibly talented."

"Well, don't keep looking at him as if you do then."

"I'm not. I've got eyes for no one but you, babe."

He snorts.

On the home front, Mika is growing fast. Sometimes I wake up in the

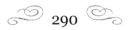

morning and find she is taller. She has grown overnight. Like me she has fallen in love with Jack. You should see the madhouse we have here when Jack comes home from work. There is barking, wailing, whining, jumping, sloppy kisses, and too many hugs.

On the fifth day something goes wrong with the heating and the apartment becomes cold. Lena tells me to go to the Kensington apartment, but I tell her I will wait for Jack to come home, and if he doesn't know what's wrong with it, we will go together. I convince her that it's not that cold since I've switched the oven on and left the door open.

However, after I put the phone down, I walk into the living room and notice a definite nip in the air, so I decide to get some blankets out and curl up with a book.

I go into the bedroom which is already freezing cold and open the cupboard. I have seen blankets stored

on the bottom shelf. I squat down and pull three out at the same time. Something hard falls with a soft thud on the floor. I pull the blankets away to see what has fallen out and notice that it is a photo album. Midnight blue with the brown cardboard showing at the edges of the cover, scratches, and finger marks.

For a few frozen seconds, I can only stare at it as if it is some alien object from outer space. Instinctively, I know it is not an ordinary album. Nobody rolls up an album in blankets and pushes it to the back of their cupboard. I can hear my ragged breathing as I bend down to pick it up.

I hold it in my hand, but I don't open it. Instead I place my finger on the finger marks. They are his. I can tell just by the size. They belong to my lover. To the man I would die for. I run my thumb along the spine.

Would it be wrong to open it?

It's not like it's a diary. It's just an album. If I owned a photo album would I be okay with him seeing it? Why not? It would only contain pictures of my family.

I grasp the cover. My heart is pounding in my chest. Thump. Thump. Thump. I lift the cover. The breath I am holding comes out in a whoosh.

Oh sweet Jesus!

I turn the pages slowly. Page by page. In a daze. Disbelief rolling in my veins. How stupid I've been. How blind. Of course. It was there for all to see. I just didn't want to. A ripple of disgust runs through me. My hands are shaking with shock as I turn the last page and close the album.

I sit on the floor and carefully roll the album back in the blanket. Then I put it back exactly where I found it. I place the other clothes back onto the shelf on top of it. I look at it. Hmmm … the red blanket was on top of the blue one. I restore the order of it. Yes, that is how I found it.

I close the cupboard door and stand up.

The sense of loss is so acute that for an instant I feel faint, but it passes. I wipe my hands down my jeans. As if they are sweaty or dirty. They are neither. They are like icicles, but I don't feel cold.

My mind is whirling in the way a gust of wind will carry a few leaves round and round. Oh God. Oh God. My sister's trigger was seeing my burnt flesh. Here is my trigger. Looking into Jack's past.

I walk out of the bedroom and go into the living room. My heart hurts. So fucking bad. I never felt this even when I was Valdislav's whore. Then I felt nothing. Nothing. I was empty. Nothing could touch me. Time had stopped then. I want to feel that way again. I want time to stop again. This is unbearable. I can't take this pain. It hurts too much. I need it to stop. I run out of the apartment without a coat.

I remember my legs shaking.

I remember stepping into the street.

There is a buzz in my head.

It is already dark. My fingers are numb. A woman passes me. She is wearing a blue coat and doesn't even see me. I envy her. It is obvious she is hurrying to a warm home and someone who loves her. She has never been a dirty prostitute. She doesn't wake up screaming. She doesn't know the meaning of the word bleak.

People walk past me. I'm invisible to all of them. I get onto a bus and hear people talking around me. All their lives are better than mine. My leg shakes restlessly. The pain is beginning to nest inside me. Like a bird bringing twigs and branches and weaving them into a solid bowl. Tears trickle out of me, but I want to howl. Like Lena did when she saw my back. I want to howl out the pain.

"Are you all right?" the bus conductor asks.

"I need to vomit," I mutter.

He calls out to the driver to stop the bus. I stumble off and hurl by the side of the road. The bus drives on. Vaguely I note the rough feel of the side of the building against which my palm rested as I stood there alone hurling my guts out.

"I'm cold," I whisper to myself as a shiver goes through me.

I should have worn my coat. I think of Jack. The way he gripped my body this morning as we slept. The way he stroked my hair. The way he entered me. The way he shot his cum into me.

I sob until my body heaves.

And you know what? So many people pass by, but not a single person stops. No one wants to interfere. No one wants to get involved. A woman without a coat in February. She must be mad. I take a tissue out of my pocket and wipe my face. I look around me.

I can't focus properly. Things look blurry. I shouldn't have fallen in love with him. Lena was right. I should have held a tiny bit of myself back.

I walk to the next bus stop and catch another bus. I know where I'm going. I know what I want. I want time to stop. I want to feel no pain. I'm tired of life. I just want peace. I don't want to care anymore. And I know how to get that empty nothing.

Thirty-six

Jack

https://www.youtube.com/watch?v=S4kzGhDEURA
(If Tomorrow Never Comes)

The key scratches in the lock as I swing it in a panic. I fling open the door and stride through the empty hallway. The place is freezing cold. I throw open the bedroom door, and in the eerie silence I see it all in one beautiful, strange, terrifying, depressing, sordid, heartbreaking glance.

There is my heart, my love, my life: Sitting on her bed. Frozen. Fragile. The soft glow from the bedside lamp illuminates one side of her face. She is wearing a white blouse under a cream sweater and blue jeans. There are two dark smudges on her sweater. My dazed mind wonders how they got there.

Her hair is pulled back into one braid down her back, but strands have escaped and hang around her face and neck. Her eyes are red and swollen. She's been crying.

There is a spoon and a candle burning on the bedside table. A telephone cord is tied around her arm. In her small hand she is holding a syringe.

If I had been a few seconds later it would have been too late. That squalid needle would be already in her arm. My stomach churns.

"What are you doing here?" she asks, her voice calm and devoid of emotion. As if we are strangers. As if I have interrupted her while she was icing a cake, or sewing a button back on a garment. I don't recognize her and it chills me to the bone.

I step towards her. I don't want to scare her.

She stares at me without expression. At this moment I'm the only one who can protect her. The only one who can shield her from the claws of the past. She stares at me with wide open eyes. I reach her and stand down looking at her. She reminds me of a little animal. Maybe a fawn. Utterly innocent. Pitiful. This cruel world has betrayed her. Cut her. Fed on her. Put tears in her eyes.

God, I love her so much I want to kill everyone who has ever hurt her. She looks so lost. She bends her head exposing her nape, the tiny bones that press against her smooth skin. The sight hurts me. I'll heal her. I will put her back together. I'll wrap her legs around me and fill her body with love.

"Why?" I ask her, my voice is a shocked whisper.

She looks up. A look of terrible pain etched on her face. For an eternity we stare into each other's eyes. The world stops spinning. There is only this moment suspended in time. Then a

tension enters her shoulders. Something passes in her eyes. Somewhere inside me a warning bell goes off.

Sofia

I look into his eyes and see the most beautiful man I have ever laid eyes on. Look at him. In the light from the lamp he is shining like a God. Pure and perfect. Magnificent. Such a man is not for me. He stands there ferocious with purpose. He thinks he can rescue me. He can never do that.

No one can. How can I ever forget what has been done to me? I'm tainted and dirty. He should have a clean woman. A woman who will bear him children and walk proudly next to him without fear of being recognized as a whore.

For I know that one day I will walk into a room and a leering stranger will say, "I've seen you. I've seen a video of you. You were the star of the show. How they all bathed you in their cum." Jack will cringe. He will be ashamed of me. Or maybe an old customer will recall how he fucked me up the ass.

No, I won't plant another day for us to hobble into. I'll end it today. I'll be brave. I'll disgust him so much he will run away from me for good. I know exactly how to do it too.

Jack

In slow motion she lifts her hand, her knuckles white, and offers the syringe to me.

I look into her beautiful eyes.

Oh Sofia, Sofia, Sofia. My enchanted, harmful fairytale.

I bend my body and she flinches with an ancient fear.

"Shhh ... don't be afraid of me, Sofia. I'll never hurt you." I smile at her.

She doesn't smile back.

I fluff the pillows and gently push her back towards them. She resists for a second then allows me to rest her head on the pillows. She looks up at me. Uncertain what I am up to.

The tantalizing smell of her shampoo fills my nostrils as I take the syringe from her unresisting hand. I untie the cord from her arm. Then I go around the other side of the bed and lie down beside her. Looking deep into her eyes I roll up my sleeves. She stares at me confused.

Then her eyes widen.

I tie the cord hard around my upper arm. She swallows hard. I take the syringe from the bed.

She opens her mouth. "No," she cries hoarsely, her voice filled with horror. As if all she thought she was dreaming and only now has realized that it is not a dream.

I run my finger down her cheek. Pure silk. "I want to. Mortality is just a game," I tell her.

Tears splash on my arm. Hers. Fetched from a well of sorrow. "I'm so sorry," she sobs. She clutches at my arm. "I didn't mean it. You are pure and beautiful. It will destroy you."

"I want to."

"Why?"

"Because I want to know what I am fighting. What I'm competing against. What is so wonderful that you will choose it over me. I want you to know there is no depth I will not go to rescue you. I'd rather take this poison into my own body than see it go into yours."

She starts crying softly. She never thought I'd take it this far.

"It will destroy you. I don't want to destroy you."

I tap the inside of my elbow, then I take the needle, push it into my vein and release the drug into it.

Sofia

I stare at him in a daze. I want to stop him, but the scene playing out in front of me is so sudden, so unexpected, it seems unreal. I watch the liquid drain into his arm. This cannot be real.

This is Jack. Big, strong Jack. The Jack that everybody loves.

Oh God! What have I done? Everybody is going to be so angry with me. I see his eyes start to glaze. And the guilt slams into me. My hand claps over my mouth.

Oh my God!

He can die!

He is not used to it. It could be too much. He could overdose. With shaking hands I pull the needle out of his arm. I need to call someone. I need to call Guy. He will know what to do. I need my phone. I try to stand, but Jack's hand shoots out and curls around my wrist. I look at his hand. He should be so out of it by now that he should have no strength, but his grip is very tight.

"Don't go," he says thickly, his eyes intense. His pupils so large and his eyes so shiny I start to shake with fear.

"I'm going to get some help for you," I explain.

"Stay. I don't need help from anyone. I only need you. I did this for you. So you'd know what it feels like when the person you love is doing this."

"What if the dose is too strong for you?"

"Nothing is stronger than my love for you. I'll go anywhere, do anything for you. As long as you're next to me nothing can destroy me. Cover us so that you're warm then put your sweet head on my chest and wait for me."

I pull the duvet over our bodies, then I put my cheek on his chest and with heat from his body seeping into my cold body and his steady heartbeat in my ear, I wait for him.

He said, when the person you love!
The person you love!
Could it be? Could it really be?

Thirty-seven

Sofia

I hold him for the next thirty-five minutes. We say nothing until he whispers, "That was fucking crap, Sofia. It's got nothing for you or me."

"It took away the pain," I whisper guiltily.

"There's no pain for you. There is nothing that my love can't overcome, Princess."

I lift my head and stare deeply into his eyes, still unable to believe the words. "You love me?"

"With all my heart and soul."

"But what about Lana?"

He frowns. "Lana? That's what this is all about? Fucking hell, Sofia. Yes, I was secretly in love with her, but I was just a boy then. She hooked up with

Blake, and sure it was difficult, but I got over it. A long time ago."

"So that was what Lana meant when she said you surprised her twice. That she never really knew you."

"No she never really knew me. I didn't show her the real me. Only you have seen the real me."

He looks at me curiously. "Who told you about Lana?"

"I wasn't snooping or anything like that, but I was cold, so I went to get some blankets from the cupboard and," I swallow hard, "I found your photo album. Every single photograph is just her."

He sighs, his eyes are disappointed. "And that was enough to condemn me?"

"All those photographs. You must have been obsessed with her."

"She was my first love, Sofia," he says, shaking his head. "And I loved her with the desperate passion of a teenager, but people do grow up and get over their first loves. I did."

I bite my lip. I so much want to believe him. "I remembered that you didn't want to kiss her at the Christmas Eve party. If you didn't have feelings for her anymore you would have."

"I didn't do it for three reasons. First, I don't kiss other men's women. Second, she is like my sister now. Her son is my godson, I have come to care about Blake, and the last thing in the world I want to do is something that would make it weird for any of us. Third, you have to be a moron to even want to go to a place that caused you nothing but pain."

Relief pours into my body, instantly chasing away all those dark thoughts.

"Why couldn't you have waited for me to come home and asked me instead of running to Andrew for a packet of smack?" he asks gently.

"I'm not like you, Jack. Bad things have happened to me and I fought for so long that I'm brittle. One little knock and I shatter. When I found the album I

thought everything we had was a lie, and without you my life felt meaningless."

"I didn't live in a vacuum before you came. There will be other things that will come up. You have to learn to trust me. To come to me confident in the knowledge that nothing is more important to me than you."

"How did you know I got the drugs from Andrew?"

"He called me to apologize. He knows better than to sell drugs to my girl."

"I'm sorry I embarrassed you."

He grasps my wrists. "You didn't embarrass me. Nothing about you embarrasses me. But something about you hurts me deeply."

"What?" I whisper.

"You never tell me anything about your past. You don't have to give me any gory details but tell me something. I feel locked out from such a big part of you."

I sigh. "It's not that I want to lock you out, but almost everything that

happened in my childhood is fraught with pain and guilt."

"Then tell me about something that's not fraught with pain. Tell me about your mother."

I take a deep breath. "When I was younger sometimes when my father was being cruel to my mother I wanted to interfere. I wanted to stop him, but I never did. I was weak." My voice begins to tremble and he wraps his arms around me and holds me tightly against his body.

"It's okay, my love. I don't need to know any of that. I just want to love you. That's all."

"There's one last thing I haven't told you that I really should have that first night."

He pushes me away from his body and smiles. "Come on then, let's hear the next great reason I shouldn't be with you."

I don't return his smile. "Valdislav made videos of me ... with more than

one man. What if, one day, someone who has watched them comes up to us and says something?"

"Two things will happen. One, he'll be due for an immediate visit to a qualified orthodontist. If he's interested I can recommend a few excellent ones. Two, I'll fucking love you even more."

I stare at him hardly daring to breathe. "You won't be ashamed of me?"

"Ashamed? What the fuck are you talking about? That's the last thing I feel. Hell, I'm so proud of you I want to shout from the rooftops that you're mine."

"Why? I'm nothing special."

He shakes his head slowly. "I could never describe how special you are to me. Just like the bird can never tell the fish how it feels to have the wind in its wings."

I stare at him. It's almost too good to be true.

"I'm that song you've never sung, Sofia. You don't know the notes we can reach together. Try me. I promise you will never regret it."

"What about kids?"

"What about them?"

"What will we tell them?"

"We'll teach our children well so that one day if we have to tell them they will be filled with nothing except great love and compassion for their brave mother."

Tears begin to roll down my cheeks.

He pulls me into his arms. "There is nothing we cannot beat together. Nothing. You hear me, Sofia Seagull. Absolutely nothing."

Thirty-eight

Jack

"God gave men a penis and a brain, but unfortunately
not enough blood supply to run both at the same time."
 - Robin Williams (1951-2014)

I arrange to take her to meet my mother. She dresses in a black and green dress which she believes is formal and conservative.

"How do I look?" she asks anxiously.

I don't tell her that I find it mind-numbingly distracting. She is wearing stockings for later and I can see the slight bulge through the material that clings to her thighs. I know exactly what I will be doing later.

"Very formal."

"Do you think it is too formal?" she worries instantly.

"No. It's just perfect."

"Are you sure?"

"Absolutely."

She smooths the skirt over her thighs with her hands and the fasteners bulge out again. My cock twitches restlessly. I'd kill to take her to bed right now, but she's too wound up.

"You'd tell me if I was over-dressed, wouldn't you?" she asks anxiously.

My eyes trail reluctantly from her thighs up to her eyes. "Absolutely."

"Are you taking the piss, Jack Irish?"

I grin. "I wouldn't dare."

She looks at me earnestly. "This is very important to me. I want to make a good impression."

"Don't worry, Princess. She'll love you."

"How can you be sure, though?"

"My mother's been nagging me to bring a girl home for years."

"When was the last time you brought a girl home?"

I shrug. "Never."

"Really?"

"Yup."

"Are there any topics I should avoid, or any last minute advice of how to handle her?"

I think about it. "Don't say anything bad about Bon Jovi."

She smiles. "Bon Jovi?"

I raise my eyebrows. "She's frighteningly passionate about him."

"Anything else?"

"She loves her home. I've tried to get her out of it into a bigger place in a better address, and she has consistently refused so say something nice about it if you can."

She nods solemnly, her brow creased in concentration. Anyone would think I was giving her the keys to a kingdom.

"Oh, and compliment her on her cooking. She likes that."

"Okay. What else?"

"Do your Irish accent impersonation."

"Are you sure she won't be insulted?"

I grin. "She'll be a fan for life."

Sofia

We climb up two flights of stairs and walk along an open corridor to reach Jack's mother's apartment. Jack looks down at me.

"Relax," he says.

I smile nervously. I don't know why I am so terrified she won't like me.

Jack puts his key in the door and opens it. The air is warm and filled with delicious smells.

"We're here," he calls out.

Almost instantly a woman pops her head around what must be the living room door. Her eyes are blue, a lighter shade than her son's, and kind. She is grinning like a child, and I lose all my nervousness. This is the woman who bore Jack. Who loves Jack and wants only the best for him. I'll show that nobody can love him more, or give him more than I can.

"What a pretty little thing you are," she says walking into the cramped hallway. She is dressed in a pretty blue dress and there is a cameo brooch pinned to her chest. Jack told me her husband died many years ago, but she is still wearing her wedding band on her finger. Her nails are painted a rosy pink.

"Thank you," I say shyly.

She looks up at her son slyly. "I can see now why your head's turned."

"Sofia, meet my mother, Florence. Ma, meet my girl, Sofia."

She leans forward and kisses me on both cheeks. "You don't know how pleased I am to meet you, Sofia."

Jack takes my coat and she ushers me into her small living room. It's charmingly cluttered and cozy.

"What a lovely home you have, Mrs. Irish."

"Call me Flo, dear. Jack told me your mother's passed on, so I'm like a mother to you from now on." Genuine warmth radiates out of her kind face.

"Thank you, Flo."

She gestures towards one of the chintz sofas. "Will you have a glass of sherry?"

"I could murder a glass."

She smiles. "Something tells me we're going to get along just fine."

I smile back. "I think so too."

After that the evening becomes a night of laughter, reminiscences from the past, and wonderful food. Florence has made lamb leg flavored with garlic and rosemary.

As we eat she tells me that in spring wild garlic appears all across Ireland in the shaded woodland areas. During that time even the air would smell of garlic. When she was a girl she used to harvest the leaves for her mother to serve with the lamb, or toss into a salad.

"Next time I will make Beef and Guinness stew. It's Jack's favorite dish. It's perfect for a cold winter's day," she says, picking up a forkful of scallion flavored, buttery mashed potato.

Dessert is Chocolate Guinness cake iced with a thick layer of creamy white chocolate and cream cheese frosting. It looks exactly like the topping on a pint of Guinness. She watches me like a hawk as I put a piece into my mouth. It is dense and fudgey with a distinctive malty flavor from the stout.

"It's completely delicious," I pronounce truthfully.

She beams happily.

Afterwards, there is coffee and little chocolates from a delicatessen down the road.

"Do your Irish impersonation," Jack urges.

"Top of the morning to you," I say loudly, and both mother and son fall about laughing.

Thirty-nine

Sofia

What a stroke of luck that on the very morning I decide to make the beef Guinness stew that Florence talked about she calls me. When I tell her I am making it from a recipe I found on a cookery blog on the net her response is predictably Florence.

"You can't trust the recipes you find on the internet. Nobody likes giving away their secrets so they'll always hold something crucial back," she says darkly.

Then she makes me get a piece of paper and gives me the recipe over the phone. She is right. While the blogger took pains to declare that browning the meat is absolutely vital as it imparts a rich flavor to the stew, she neglected to mention the real secret to browning. The

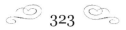

meat has to be browned as large steaks then taken out of the pan and diced. Florence tells me browning small pieces of meat will make the meat tough as leather, after which no amount of stewing will soften it.

"Do you want me to go through it all again?" she asks when we get to the end.

"Nope. I got it all, Flo. Thank you."

"Hmmm ... Make sure you get a good piece of boneless shoulder."

"I can get that at the supermarket, right?"

"Yes child."

"I will go there this afternoon"

"I forgot to say," she adds, "that like the meat, the vegetables should be browned as large pieces. Fish them out when you are nearly at the end of your cooking. After you have simmered them with the meat to get the flavor out of them, just fish them out. They will be quite soggy and tasteless by then, so you replace them with freshly diced vegetables."

"I will," I tell her, my pen scribbling fast.

"What else? What else?" she mutters to herself. "Oh yes, don't use more than two tablespoons of flour, or it will become muddied."

"I'll remember that."

"And yellow onions. Not red."

On my paper I add yellow next to the word onion. "Got it."

"Not too many parsnips, or it will overpower all the other ingredients."

"Fine." I note that down too.

"Did I say use chicken stock, not beef?"

I run my gaze down her instructions. "Err … you didn't say, but good that you mentioned it. I would have got beef."

"If I think of anything else I'll call you again," she says.

"Thank you again, Flo," I say with a smile in my heart. I think I'm going to love having her in my life. She's so genuine and real.

That afternoon Lena comes around with Irina, and we take a trip to the supermarket together. Leaving Mika in the car, we go in to get all the ingredients I need while Lena buys some stuff for herself. Afterwards, Lena stays with me for a bit. Once Irina has been changed, fed, and put down for a nap, we sit and have coffee and the cream cakes we got at the bakery.

"You are happy, aren't you?" she asks.

"Yes, very," I reply, and she grins happily.

When Irina wakes up an hour later, Lena goes back to Cheshire, and I start to make my stew. I just put all my ingredients on the counter top to begin cooking when Jack calls.

"Whatcha doing, doll?" he asks.

"Well," I say, slicing open the plastic bag of carrots, "I'm preparing a surprise for you?"

"My dick just got hard."

I laugh. "Not that type of surprise."

"What then?"

I start putting the vegetables on the chopping board. "Do you know what the word surprise means?"

"I know what the word means I'm just not a big fan. Just tell me," he coaxes persuasively.

"You can use that voice all you like. I'm not spoiling my surprise."

He sighs. "At least tell me what you're wearing."

I glance down at my thick sweater and old jeans. "The truth, or shall I make it up as I go along?"

"Make it up."

"You're one of those guys who calls up adult chat lines and listens to women pretending to climax while they're actually painting their toenails, aren't you?" I tease.

"What's with all the wild accusations? I'll have you know I've never called an adult chat line in my life. However, I could be persuaded to call one if you are going to man it."

I giggle. That's what I like about my Jack. He treats me exactly the way he would if he was with any other normal woman. I never get that with Guy or Lena. They are always walking on eggshells around me. Lena has now managed the impressive feat of never once mentioning the word whore, prostitute, or hooker for over a year.

Once while we were watching TV together, she was flicking channels and hit Pretty Woman, and you should have seen how quickly she clicked out of it. She is so hurt by my past and so frightened of hurting me that she doesn't realize it only makes my past feel even more shameful and dirty to me.

Jack on the other hand won't allow anything to come between us. He accepts my past completely and behaves as if it is a non-starter in our relationship. As far as he is concerned we're starting with a clean slate. If he has a fantasy he wants to explore with me where he leaves a thousand pounds on the bedside and pretends he is my customer, then we'll talk about it in the same way we'll talk about his fantasy of tying me to the bed, or getting me off in a public place. At every opportunity he instills in me that we're just a normal couple finding out what works for us.

"Go on," he urges, using his melted butter voice. "My next appointment is in less than ten minutes."

"Nope," I say firmly, picking up the knife. "I don't think I'm going to indulge you right now. I'm too busy preparing your surprise."

"Treat them mean and keep them keen huh?"

"Exactly."

"Fine. It better be some surprise," he says grumpily.

I end the call, still smiling, and start chopping off the heads of the carrots. Everything goes according to plan, and I had already poured in the chicken stock and Guinness over the meat and vegetables. I was just about to put the stew into the oven, when Florence calls.

"Sofia, have you started making your stew yet?"

"Yeah, I'm just about to put it into the oven."

"Oh, thank heavens. I forgot to tell you to add a small cup of strong black coffee and a piece of bittersweet chocolate."

"At what stage should I add it?"

"Now."

I laugh. "That was a bit of luck, wasn't it?"

She joins in the laughter.

I end the call and look in the fridge. I have no dark chocolate. I switch off the stove and scribble a note for Jack if he comes when I'm out.

Gone to get chocolate. Love you. xoxo

Then I grab my phone and my purse, pull on my coat and my silly purple hat because it is drizzling outside, and go to the front door. Mika whines because she wants to come, but I don't take her because it's wet and messy and I'll only be gone for a short time.

"Just wait for me. I'll be back soon," I say, and slip out of the door.

I button my coat in the elevator. As I come out of it I see the little old lady that lives in the apartment a floor below us coming through the entrance so I wait and hold the lift for her. She smiles at me.

"It's horrible out there," she sniffs.

"I know."

"I'll be glad to put my feet up with a cup of tea," she says.

I step out into the street. It is already busy with people returning from work. I huddle into my coat and hurry down the road. I get into the shop and

Kaja is behind the counter. There is no one else in the shop and she chats with me as I pay for my chocolate bar. As she is returning my change, that quaint little bell over the shop door rings.

I turn around and my heart stops.

Forty

Lena

I stand by the window staring at the needles of rain lashing the glass. I don't know why I feel restless and jittery inside. I've felt as if there is a tight knot in my stomach ever since I woke up this morning. Even Guy knew something was wrong.

My first thought was that it was something to do with Sofia, so I called her straight away, but she seemed fine. Still, I invited myself to her place. She was the picture of health. We went shopping together and even then the niggling sensation wouldn't go away, so I actually asked her outright if she was happy.

"Yes," she said, and glowed like a light bulb. You can't fake that kind of joy. That made me feel a little better.

Then, while I was there Jack called, and the way she melted at the sound of his voice made me sure there was nothing wrong.

Reassured, I came back home, but the tightness in my stomach is worse, far worse now that I have come home, and I'm alone. It must be my paranoia working overtime. Maybe I'm just not used to seeing her so happy. I know Jack is ridiculously in love with her, but a part of me is still frightened that it is all too fabulous. That something bad is looming on the horizon.

I touch my forehead. Or, maybe I'm just coming down with something. I see Mary's reflection appear in the glass, turn around and smile at her.

"Would you like me to bring in some tea?" she asks.

"No, thank you, Mary. I had a cup with Sofia."

"Oh, how is she today?"

My mouth curves automatically. "She's fine. She's cooking for her man tonight."

"It's good to know that she's happy. She has a beautiful heart."

"Yes, she does." I turn towards the glass and the rain splattering on it. "Why don't you have an early night, Mary? Make your way back to the village before the storm comes."

"I will. Thank you, Mrs. Hawke."

"Good night."

"Good night."

She leaves the room and I turn back to the window. It is dark and miserable. Lightning streaks across the sky. The weather is definitely going to get much worse. Strange to have a thunderstorm in winter. I remember when I first arrived at this house, how a big tree came down in the night. I hope no trees come down tonight. It's always a sad occasion for me when we lose a tree.

"Lena."

I whirl around in surprise. The room is empty but for me, but I could have sworn I heard Sofia's voice call my name. I freeze and listen, but there is only the sound of the rain. The kitchen is too far for sounds to carry, and Irina is upstairs with her nanny.

My heart starts beating really fast.

The churning sensation in my stomach is so strong I feel physically sick. I press my hand into my belly. Something *is* wrong. Very wrong. I know it. I run to the table, grab my phone, and call Sofia.

It rings out.

I call her home phone. Sometimes she'll leave her cellphone somewhere and not hear it from the kitchen.

There is no answer.

The knot in my stomach is so tight I can barely breathe when I call Jack.

Forty-one

Jack

I write a note for Karen in the file of the patient sitting in front of me, close it, and look up at her with a smile. "If you take this outside my assistant will sort out some dates for you."

"Thank you very much, Doc," she says taking the thin folder from me.

"No problem." I stand and start walking around the table.

She follows my example and we walk together towards the door. I open the door and hold my hand out. As she puts hers in it my phone starts ringing.

"Saved by the bell," she quips.

I smile politely. "See you soon," I say, letting go of her hand.

As soon as she walks through the door I close it, cross the room, and glance at my phone. It's Lena. With a frown I accept the call.

"What's up, Lena?"

"Do you know where Sofia is?" she asks in a rush.

"At home," I say immediately, even though my brain instantly registers that she can't be or Lena wouldn't be calling me.

"She's not. I've tried both her mobile and the landline. She's not answering either." Her voice is high and full of anxiety.

At that point my mind refuses to believe anything could be wrong. I am very aware that Lena tends to be overprotective. "She should be," I say mildly. "She said she was preparing a surprise for me. I assumed she was cooking something."

"She was, but I can't contact her, Jack, and I'm really worried. I know it sounds stupid to you, but something is wrong. I can feel it."

Her words send a chill through my body. "I'm on my way," I say striding towards my door.

I run through the reception and burst out into the street in my shirt. I run around the block to where my car is parked. I get into my car and start the engine. A text comes through. It is Lena again.

Please call me the instant you find her.

I turn on the ignition and speed dial Sofia's number. Sofia has never activated her answerphone and it rings out. I swing out into the traffic, swearing.

The journey home is without any doubt the longest one I have ever taken. I get cursed at by a dozen irate drivers, but fuck them. I just use the sheer width of my Lambo to literally ram my way through the traffic.

They honk and viciously spit profanities at me, but they make way. I don't care what happens to my steel box, but they do. I hit two red lights and just plough through, but less than a block away from home I get stuck in a standstill traffic jam. I pull over onto double yellow lines, get out, and start running.

I fly through the entrance door of my building and slam my palm on the elevator button. It opens. I go in and pace the floor restlessly while I wait for the elevator to take me up to my floor.

The doors swish open and I run down the corridor. On the other side of the door I can hear Mika barking, and for a few seconds I actually think everything is fine. She must have popped out and now she is back with the dog. Fucking hell, Sofia. This is some surprise all right. I open the door and Mika doesn't run in mad circles around me. Instead she barks in a high pitched tone.

Oh shit.

I rush through the apartment calling for her, even though I know she is not there. In the kitchen I see the half-cooked pot of stew. I touch the pot and it is still warm. The oven light is on.

I look around and see her hastily scribbled note stuck under a fridge magnet. I stride up to it and snatch it off the fridge. She went to get chocolate. I dial her number, and as it rings I walk through the apartment. At least I know the phone is not here. She took it with her.

I run all the way to the corner shop. Kaja must have seen me running because she comes out and stands under the awning at the entrance of her shop. Her hands are tightly clutching the edges of her cardigan and her eyes are anxious.

"Have you seen Sofia?" I ask urgently.

She nods, her hands coming up to gesture wildly as words tumble out of her quickly. "Yes, she came here. She

bought chocolate and then these two scary men came in. They spoke to her. I think in Russian. She didn't say anything to them. She just turned to me, and asked me if she could leave a message for you with me. She looked pale and strange. Not like herself at all. She was talking like a robot. I was so shocked I just nodded and she said, 'Tell Jack. I'll love him to the day I die.' Then she went with them."

I stare at Kaja in horror. I had imagined her falling, hurting herself, lying in a hospital with a fractured leg, even a concussion, but never this.

"I'm so sorry. I didn't know what to do. They called her by name and she went with them willingly so I couldn't even call the police, but they were big and had dangerous eyes."

"How long ago was this?" I demand
She glances at her wristwatch. "Exactly ... twenty-seven minutes ago."

"Can you describe them?"

"Yes," she says, and immediately starts describing them in astonishing detail. "Both of them were wearing black leather jackets and very shiny black shoes. One was wearing blue jeans with a white shirt. He had a short, red beard, small pale blue eyes, a broken nose, and his hair was cut close to his head. He was big, even bigger than you and thick around the middle. The other one had black hair, black eyes, a scar here," her hand points to the apple of her right cheek, "and he was clean shaven. He was wearing a dark blue shirt and black jeans. He was shorter and narrower."

"Do you know which way they went?"

"That way." She immediately points in the opposite direction I had come from.

I look in the direction she pointed not really expecting to see anything, but I see the type of plastic bags that Kaja uses in her shop caught between the black metal cover and the bin inside. It is fluttering in the wind like a flag. Even from where I am standing I can tell that there's still something inside it. I dash over to it and yank it.

There is a bar of dark chocolate in it.

"That's the bar she bought," Kaja says next to me.

I turn to look at her. Her eyes are wide and scared.

I take my phone out of my pocket and hit Sofia's number. I close my eyes when I hear her phone ringing from inside the bin. I want to roar with fury. They took her. They just came and took her.

They fucking took *my* woman. My heart. Why the fuck did I not see this coming? I should have known. I should have protected her better.

Beside me Kaja speaks. "We should call the police."

Forty-two

Sofia

https://www.youtube.com/watch?v=W
rZ9rHFwGY

I don't feel anything.

I sit at the back of the car completely numb and detached. There is no desire in me to do anything. I don't try to signal the drivers of other cars that I am being kidnapped. Even though my hands are not bound I don't try to open the doors, or try to slam my shoes into the backs of Gorky's and Bogdan's heads.

Gorky is driving and Bogdan is smoking a cigarette. He has the window open and cold air rushes into the car. They are so relaxed because they know I will never do anything. I have been

345

warned that if I do anything stupid Jack will suffer the consequences.

Once at a traffic light stop, a sweet kid with pigtails in the backseat of a SUV grins and waves at me. I just stare at her blankly. I watch as the smile dies on her little face and some part of me feels bad. Our car pulls away and she's gone forever.

I guess, I always knew it was too good to last.

The holiday is over. I'm going back to Valdislav.

There is a lot of rush hour traffic on the road and it takes more than an hour to arrive at our destination. Gorky parks the car on the side of the road and we walk up the path to an end of terrace house with a walled garden. They knock on the front door and a very large, unsmiling bald man I don't recognize opens it.

"What took you so long?" he barks.

"Traffic," Bogdan says.

"He's waiting for you."

Inside it smells like every brothel I have been to. Perfume and sex. A young woman in shorts and a halter top comes out of a doorway hung with transparent blue curtains. She looks at me then immediately ducks back into the room she had exited.

Through the transparent veils I can see a living room with red couches. We don't go into it. We take the stairs and go into an L-shaped corridor. There are five doors and they are all closed. They lead me to the farthest one. Gorky knocks and I hear the voice I prayed I'd never hear again.

Gorky opens the door and gives me a slight push.

It is a room like many I have seen before. It has a flogging cross, and the bed has metal implements attached to it.

There is a cage in one corner of the room. Yes, I have been in such a room many times before.

He is standing by the window smoking a cigarette. The window is open and soft breezes are blowing in, making the curtains billow. He turns his face and looks at me.

He looks exactly the same. His hair is full of gel and his eyes are dark and hot and cruel, but I'm not afraid. I will never be afraid again. Someone truly *loves* me. I stare at him blankly. *Whatever you do to my body, you will never be able to take that away, because he taught me that. I am more than anything you do to my body.*

All the things you did to my body, and yet you could never ruin me. Never. I was beautiful to Jack.

"Hello, Sofia," he drawls. His voice is like sandpaper.

I say nothing.

"Go," he tells the men.

They close the door. The dark brown carpet swallows their footsteps.

"You look well," he notes.

I don't reply.

"Have you missed me?" he asks.

I shake my head.

He raises an eyebrow. "Not even a tiny bit?"

I shake my head again.

His mouth twists, half sarcastic, half self-deprecating. I've never seen him like this. He was always so brutal and unforgiving. The least mistake and … I shiver.

"Well," he confesses. "I missed you. A lot. I should never have sold you. It was a mistake. You're mine."

Automatically my head shakes. I don't belong to him. I never did. I belong to Jack and only Jack.

Anger flashes in his eyes. "Take your clothes off," he orders harshly.

I stare at him.

"I said take your fucking clothes off," he screams, and I jump with an old

349

fear. Something inside me clicks into place. Jack is no longer here to protect me. My chest becomes a nest and memories fly in to roost like blackbirds. The hidden past comes back to life. How could I have forgotten?

Cowering between his legs. Choking on his dick. Tears streaming down my face. All while he holds my nose and spits on me. My eyes popping. My lungs bursting. Fainting on the cold floor of his bedroom. Then being kicked into consciousness.

Bravery is for the inexperienced. A baby will crawl curiously towards a brightly colored snake, or try to catch an open flame because it doesn't understand the danger.

I have suffered the poison and experienced the burn.

My eyes dart to his free hand. It is relaxed and tapping against his thigh. Slowly, I lift my hands up. They feel so heavy. I take my coat off and let it drop to the floor. I take off my silly purple hat, my baggy sweater, my T-shirt, my shoes, my black jeans, and the new underwear that I had planned to surprise Jack with. The cold air from the window makes my skin prickle with goose bumps.

He sucks at his cigarette and lets his eyes rove over my body greedily. When he exhales, smoke veils his eyes.

"You were living with a man?"

I nod.

"Don't act like a fool, Sofia. Speak up," he orders, barely holding onto his irritation.

I flinch. It's so cold I have started shivering. I clench my teeth to keep them from chattering. "How did you find me?" I ask.

His mouth curves cruelly. "Little fool. You attended a *Bratva* wedding. Someone recognized my whore all dressed up like royalty." He flicks his cigarette butt out of the open window and turns to face me. "Haven't I told you before, you're not a normal woman, sweet Sofia? You're a whore. A prostitute. Your lot in life is not to marry and have kids and get fat. Your lot is to pleasure men. Lots of men ... while I watch."

I shake my head. "No. No, I'm not a whore."

His eyes narrow and his voice is taunting. "You didn't tell him what you were, did you?"

"He knows," I say defensively.

He laughs a maniacal sound that seems to echo around us. "Then you won't mind that he'll be getting a naughty little surprise in his post box tomorrow? Hmmm."

My body becomes rigid with horror. "No. Please. Don't. Please," I beg.

"What's the matter, my little whore? Don't you want him to see how talented you are? How many cocks you can service at the same time. It's been so long even I have forgotten. How many, Sofia?"

"Please don't. Please."

"If you don't do exactly what I want he will get the videos. I'm feeling generous so I might even give him a box set."

"I'll do whatever you want."

"Good. Now answer me. How many men can you service at the same time?"

"Five," I cry. "Five."

"He doesn't know that, does he?"

I shake my head. Tears are pouring from my eyes. My teeth are chattering and my skin is getting red.

"Turn around," he orders.

There. There is that first jolt of real fear.

"Go on," he says silkily.

Slowly, my feet turn. My heart is pounding so hard I feel faint. For what feels like eternity there is absolutely no sound in the room but the blood roaring in my ears. Then I hear his footsteps cross the room.

"Well, well, my masochistic whore," he murmurs against my hair. "I guess I'll have to mark you all over again."

Forty-three

Jack

https://www.youtube.com/watch?v=vo
nmHymgM7Y
(I'm Ready, My Lord)

I look at either side of the street in a kind of helpless daze. My mind is a blank. I can't think. It feels like I am in a dream. Unreal, slow moving, terrifying. There's a monster coming for you. You can hear its dragging footsteps, but you're immobilized. A sitting duck shaking with dread.

Kaja is saying something else, but I can't make out the words.

"We should call the police," she repeats, raising her voice.

Cold rain falls on my face and soaks through my shirt. Kaja is looking at me anxiously and people are staring at us, but I can't do a thing. I'm just frozen with panic. Inside me things are shattering. My skin is crawling with horror and revulsion. I clench my hair on either side of my head while my world narrows around me. This can't be fucking happening.

Something starts ringing. For a couple of seconds I don't even recognize what the sound is.

"Your phone," Kaja shouts.

My phone. I fumble in my jacket, lay my hands on it and pull it out. The rain is in my eyes and I have to squint at the screen to see it. Lena. On autopilot I press reply and put the phone to my ear.

"Have you found her yet?" she asks.

The urgency and worry in her voice is like a bolt of lightning in a dark sky. I snap out of my crazy descent into hell. My voice when it comes out is hoarse. "Not yet. I'm just going to look for her."

"Why do you mean you're going to look for her?" she cries. Her voice is so shrill it goes right through me.

"Lena. Just sit tight and let me find her, okay. I'll call you as soon as I have some information."

Lena is still saying something in that same borderline hysterical voice, but I kill the connection. I can't deal with her right now. I need to find Sofia. I need to think. I turn to Kaja. Her hair is plastered to her head and she is staring at me worriedly.

"Go back to your shop, Kaja. I'll find her."

"Are you sure?"

I nod.

Yeah, I'm fucking sure. They messed with the wrong fucking man.

Kaja touches my arm and turns away. I call Guy.

"Yes," he says briskly.

"Sofia has been kidnapped." My voice is hard and emotionless.

"What?" he explodes.

"It looks like she's been taken by the men you bought her from."

"How do you know that?"

I take a deep breath. "Just go with my instinct, Guy. I haven't got much time. Can you tell me everything you know about them?"

"Give me a few minutes, I'll make some calls," he says, and hangs up.

I scroll through my address book and hit the number for Noah Abramovich. I never thought I'd ever need a favor from him.

"Jack," his deep voice says on the second ring. "What can I do for you?"

"I'm looking for a Russian brothel owner called Valdislav."

"Valdislav?" he repeats incredulously. "What do you want with him?"

"He has my woman and I want her back."

There is a slight pause. "You have to give me some backstory to this."

"I don't have much time so here's the short version. She used to belong to him. Then he sold her to her sister's husband, but for whatever reason he sent two men to steal her back this afternoon."

"I see." There is a short pause. "Valdislav has a brothel in King's Cross, but if he has kidnapped her he will take her to his unofficial parlor in Tower Bridge. That place is more secure and hardly anyone knows of its existence. You will have to move fast because he probably won't keep her in this country long. His influence here is weak so he will try to move her back to his little fiefdom in Brussels at the first opportunity. He has bought the protection of the local cops and getting her back from there will be a whole lot harder."

"Give me the address of his brothel here."

"You cannot go there on your own, it's too well guarded. Wait until later

tonight and I will arrange for some men to go with you."

My brain picks up on an oddity. "Why would they strongly guard a brothel?"

"It's a place for specialist perversions. The women in there are all trafficked. For the right price you can even kill them during your session."

"Fuck. I'm not waiting for one fucking second more. Just give me the address," I shout.

"Jack, you have no idea what you are dealing with. These people are ruthless. They'll kill you." His voice is hard and final.

"Whatever. Just give me the address."

"That would be stupid. You're taking a knife to a gun fight."

I frown. "How do you know I carry a knife?"

"Have you forgotten, Jack? My men followed you around for months after you rescued me. Please. Give me a

chance to come up with a workable plan. I promise you it will be done tonight."

"Once I saved your life. You said if I even needed help all I had to do was ask. I'm asking now, you owe me this favor. Give me his address and we are quits."

He tries to dissuade me a little longer, but I am so adamant and impatient he reluctantly gives it to me.

"Now tell me as much as you can about this place and the security system," I say.

"I don't know that much about it. Give me five minutes and I'll call you back with as much information as I can get."

"Thanks. Oh, can you text me a photo of him."

"Sure."

I walk back to my apartment completely cold and calm inside. I don't think about Sofia, because that will only make me weak. I think about exactly what I have to do, and I try to lay my plan as meticulously as possible. With a plan B for every eventuality.

Once inside our home, I switch off the oven. Mika whines pitifully at my heels. I pick her up, look into her innocent eyes, and feel a stab of pain. I may never see this sweet dog again. I stroke her head and tip food into her bowl. All the while my mind is swirling with ideas on how best to proceed.

Forty-four

Jack

My phone rings. It's Guy.

"Yes," I reply.

"There's not much I could find. He has a brothel here in London, but as far as everyone knows he is still in Belgium. I have people working flat out to try and find out more."

"Okay, let me know if you get any more information."

"Shouldn't we call the police?"

"Not yet. Call the police if I don't contact you by the morning."

"Jack, what are you planning?"

"I haven't got time to explain, Guy."

"Do you need me to do anything?"

"No. Just come around in the morning and take Mika back to Lena if you don't hear from me by then. I'll leave the key under the mat. I've got another call coming through, I've got to go."

I get rid of Guy and accept Noah's call.

"Tell me," I say, walking into my bedroom.

"There are at least two pitbulls and a rottweiler patrolling the grounds, and three to four highly trained men on the premises at any given time. Business doesn't pick up until a bit later so there will be girls, but probably no more than one or two johns for the next couple of hours. There is a closed-circuit security system and cameras in every room. The chance of you getting in and out alive are zero."

I let the comment pass, kill the call, and phone my friend Harry, the vet. We went to school together. I haven't seen him in years, but he used to hero worship me. He was a grade A kid and I was the cool gangster.

"JackfuckingIrish," he says. "What's going on with you, my man?"

"Are you still at work?" I ask as I strip my wet clothes off.

"I'm married to the job, man," he says with a laugh.

"Can I come around for some supplies?"

"Supplies?"

"Tell you when I get there."

"Mi casa, Su casa," he says with a laugh.

I cut the connection and call my mother.

"What you doing, Ma," I ask as I grab a towel and start drying myself.

"Cleaning the downstairs cupboard. You won't believe the rubbish I've been hoarding. I've still got stuff from your schooling days."

"Yeah?" I can almost see her. Wearing her apron and her blue rubber gloves. Her hair tied back in a scarf.

"Did the stew turn out good?" she asks.

My hand clenches. "I don't know. It's not ready yet."

"Did she manage to get the chocolate?"

My heart contracts. "Yeah, I think so."

"Good. It's a good thing I remembered in time."

"Thanks for helping Sofia, Ma." I throw the wet towel into the washing basket and, naked, head for the cupboard.

"Awww. I love that girl. When are you going to put a ring on her finger?"

I swallow the lump. "As soon as I can, Ma. As soon as I can."

"She's a good girl."

I die a little inside at the injustice of life. "I got to go now, Ma. I just called to see that you were all right and to thank you for everything."

"Thank me for what?"

"For being so kind to Sofia. For treating her like your own daughter."

"Don't be talking nonsense now," she says gruffly.

"Bye, Ma."

"Bye son."

"Ma?"

"I love you."

"Oh, Jack. I love you too."

I terminate the call and open my wardrobe door. My last will and testament is all in order, and everything will go to her. She will be a rich woman. Not that she will want it. I guess she can give it all away.

A text comes through. It's a photo of Valdislav. I look at him, my stomach filling with acid. Hate surges into me. I stare at him for a moment longer. The sly eyes, the self-satisfied smirk. We will meet soon, you sick bastard. Very soon. Then we'll see how you smirk.

Then I click out of it. My hands are completely steady and I feel utterly focused on my mission.

I dial Lana's number, and putting the phone down, step into a pair of underpants.

"Hi, Jack," she says brightly.

I sit on the bed and pull on my socks. I'm always going to love this woman. Always. "Hey, Lana. I just wanted you to know that I'll always love you. You're truly the sister I never had."

She laughs. "You're getting soft in the head, Irish. What's all this in aid of?"

"Nothing. Sometimes it's good to tell people what they mean to you."

"Well, you know exactly how I feel about you."

"I do, Lana. Anyway, is Sorab there?"

"Right here, actually, but before I put him on, want to do dinner together next week? The four of us?"

My voice doesn't falter. "Sure, why not."

"Okay. I'll arrange something and liaise with Sofia."

"Fine."

"Bye, Jack. Here is your godson now."

"Hello, Uncle Jack." His voice is bright and full of life.

"Hello, Dragon Slayer."

"Are you coming over tonight, Uncle Jack?"

"Not tonight, but I hope you're being a good boy."

"I am," he says instantly. "Uncle Jack?" His voice is full of excitement.

"Yeah."

"I'm getting a dog tomorrow from the Rescue Center."

"Wow! That's brilliant."

"He's only got three legs, but he chose me. He came up to me and licked my hand, and I knew he was for me."

For the strangest reason my eyes burn with tears. "What are you going to call him?"

"I'm going to call him Jack Double."

I close my eyes. Sorab will show this world how it is done. I will die happy knowing that a child like him exists in this world. If my only legacy will be to lend my name to a three-legged dog belonging to him, I am content.

"I've got to go, Sorab, but I want you to always remember that I'm so proud of you."

"Nite nite, Uncle Jack."

"Goodbye, Sorab."

Quickly, I get into a black turtle neck jumper and trousers. I pull my sneakers out from the bottom of my cupboard and lace them up. They are more silent than ordinary shoes.

Next, I go to my drawer and take out the knife I've had since I was a kid. Noah thinks I'm taking a knife to a gun fight, but not many people can do with a gun what I can with a knife. I slip it into the back of my jeans waistband. There is also another smaller knife in the drawer. I slip that into my right sock.

Going into the kitchen, I fish out the half-cooked meat from the stew, ladle the pieces into a plastic bag, and tie the top securely. Opening the fridge, I take out the expensive bottle of champagne that Sofia was saving for Valentine's day.

I stuff the bottle and the meat into a shopping bag.

With Mika following closely behind, I go into the living room. I pick up my phone and look up the address of Valdislav's brothel on Google Maps. It is at the end of the road in a residential area. Navigating around the neighborhood, I find that the house opposite seems to be built in exactly the same design.

I leave the key under the mat and go out to meet my fate.

Forty-five

Jack

Harry's practice is not far from Victoria Station, so I get there quite quickly using the same bully boy method I employed earlier. I don't see any traffic wardens so I brazenly park on the sidewalk outside his premises and dash inside.

He takes me to his office.

"What's going on?" he asks.

"I haven't got the time to explain, Harry."

"Fine. What do you need?"

"I need tranquilizers. Give me enough to put four men down."

His eyebrows shoot up into his receding hairline. "Whoa. What have you got yourself involved in?"

My impatience must have flashed in my eyes because he lifts his hands up,

palms facing me and backs off. "Don't eat me. I'll go get them for you."

"Have you got a tranquilizer gun?"

This time he turns around and stares at me. "Are you serious?"

"I need to take down at least three dogs. Two pitbulls and one rottie."

He shakes his head as if he just can't believe what he is hearing, then nods. "Yeah, I'll get it for you."

He brings them to me and gives me a quick demo on how to use the gun. He hands me the tranquilizer injections. "Use them with care. Each one is enough to bring down a very small horse or a very big man."

I slip them into my jacket pocket. "Thanks. Now can I have your coat and a nametag if you have one lying around?"

Wordlessly, he roots around in one of his drawers and finds a nametag. He takes off his white coat and gives both items to me.

I take the coat and pin the nametag on it. "Do you have a clipboard and pen?"

He puts both his hands up again as if he has quit trying to figure out what is happening and goes to a back room. He comes back with a clipboard and pen.

I take them from him and cast my eyes on the things on his table top. "Thanks. One last thing. Can I have an A4 paper with some lines or boxes on it. Something that looks like a form."

He doesn't say anything, just returns to the room at the back and comes back with a stack of forms with boxes, words and lines on it.

"Oh, and either your credit card machine or a calculator."

"No way man. I need my credit card machine, but you can have my calculator. It's out front at reception," he says, leading the way there. He reaches behind the counter and comes up with a medium sized calculator. If I'm lucky it will do.

"Brilliant. Thanks. I owe you one, Harry," I say.

"You owe me at least five," he says.

I push open his glass door and see a stony-faced traffic warden writing a ticket for my car. I run to my car and jump into it.

"Once I have issued the ticket you still have to pay it," he hollers as I roar off.

The journey to Tower Bridge takes me just under half an hour, even with me blaring my horn and acting like a total jerk.

I park the car, take my jacket off and get into Harry's white coat. Buttoning it up, I take the clipboard and the calculator, and stride confidently to the end of the road. I don't even glance at the house I am interested in. Instead, I walk to the house opposite. Thank god, there are lights on. Through the window I can see three kids sitting at a table doing their homework. I ring the bell.

A woman answers the door. "Yes?" she asks with a frown.

I look down at my clipboard first then up at her. "Good evening, Madam. There has been a gas leak in the area, and I'd like to check that your house has not been affected." I wave my calculator at her.

She stops frowning and looks alarmed. "Of course," she says, stepping back and opening the door wider.

Until this moment I never imagined it was going to be this easy. I didn't really believe the article I read that most people are so reassured with badges of authority that they would even let anyone with a clipboard or a uniform into their house without checking their identity first.

"Thank you," I say, stepping into her hallway. "This won't take long, and you can follow me around the house for your peace of mind."

"All right," she agrees immediately.

I angle the calculator so that she can only see the back of it, and start walking around her house. I note the cloakroom on my left and go into an open plan living room. The kids look up at me curiously. Holding my calculator aloft I smile politely at them and quickly walk through the room past the dining table towards the sliding glass doors.

"Can I open them?" I ask the woman.

"Of course," she says, and rushes to open it for me.

I step out into the garden and observe the measurements. I re-enter the house through the kitchen door. It's not big, but there is a side door which leads to a small pantry. I walk into the corridor that leads back to the reception rooms and the front door. There is another door to my right. I open it and find a smaller reception room. I go into it with my calculator held up high, look at it, press a few buttons, and turn around to smile at the woman.

"So far so good," I proclaim.

She smiles back, relieved. I go upstairs with the woman following me anxiously and note the exact layout of the house while pretending to monitor the gas levels.

I turn to look at her. "Looks like all is well with your house."

She appears happy.

"I'll be off then."

She follows me to the front door, and fucking thanks me for the privilege of casing her house before closing the door. If I make it through this, I'll send her a note and tell her never to let a stranger with a clipboard into her house again.

I glance at the opposite house as I walk back to my car. There are lights on in it. I chuck the clipboard into the well of the front seat and, taking off my coat, I slip quickly into my black jacket. I check that my tranquilizer injections are still in the pocket. Then I stuff the tranquilizer gun into the waistband of my jeans, take the bag with the meat and champagne, and set off down the road.

I walk around the wall of the house. When I get to the position where I cannot be seen from the road, I throw the meat over the wall and wait for the dogs to smell it.

The two pitbulls come almost instantly. They must be starving because they growl and snap at each other in their race to gobble down the fresh meat. The rottie is next to arrive. It joins in the foray.

Lifting myself over the wall I take aim and shoot. The rottie first because it is the biggest. It whines and jumps back in shock. The pitbulls carry on eating. I land back on the ground and reload. One after the other I get the pitbulls. Then I hang around for about ten minutes while the darts take effect.

The rottie is still growling softly when I jump into the enemy's yard.

Forty-six

Jack

I crouch low, and keeping in the shadows of the wall, make my way to the back door. I notice there is a window open upstairs. Good. I will climb the drainpipe if the kitchen door is locked.

I look in through the window and the kitchen is empty. I try the door and it turns. They were obviously expecting the dogs to protect this door. Very careless. A good sign. I open the door and step into the house. The microwave is on and something is slowly turning inside. I look at the display panel on it. In thirty seconds it will ping.

I pull open the side door and step into the pantry. The microwave pings. Through the slit I see a bald hulk of a man come into the kitchen. Chest to chest he might have three inches on me.

He takes his food out of the oven and opens a drawer, the engorged muscles in his meaty arms flexing. He has size but I have speed in both feet and hands.

While the three-hundred-pound gorilla is riffling for cutlery, I slip out, my body seeming to act without conscious thought when I bash him over the head with my champagne bottle. I've been in a lot of bar room brawls and nothing beats the solid weight of a champagne bottle.

Unlike the Hollywood movies where the sugar syrup bottles smash into a thousand pieces, the champagne bottle stays completely intact. There is nothing more than a dull thump when the bottle makes contact with his skull, but his massive legs give way under him and he drops to the floor. I hook my wrists under his armpits and drag him into the pantry. Quickly, I remove the plastic cover from the tranquilizer syringe, and stick the needle into his bulging arm muscles.

Strange. He has a tooth missing.

I open the door a crack. No one has come looking for him yet, but they will. I don't have much time. Carrying the champagne bottle, I slink down the corridor like a shadow. There is no one in the small reception room, but I can hear voices coming from the large main room. At least one male and two female voices. I look in through the crack of the door and see a very young woman. She can't be more than twenty.

She is wearing tight pink shorts and a bikini top. There are blue-black choke marks around her neck. One look at her and I know she's not here willingly. She is sitting on a sofa looking at the two other people speaking in the room.

I take a big risk.

I step into her vision. Her eyes widen and her mouth drops open, but I place my finger over my lips. She swallows hard. Her eyes dart first to her left then to her right, and I know instantly that the real danger is on her left. I make a beckoning motion with my hand and point upstairs. She frowns and I do it again. She nods, stands up, and adjusts her tight shorts, pulling them down.

"Candy," she says. "Can you come upstairs with me for a minute? I need you to help me with something."

"What now?" Candy asks.

"Yeah, I better do it before the customers start arriving."

"What is it?" the man asks. His voice is stern.

"I just need Candy to help me camouflage some bruises on my back with make-up. I just remembered I got Anderson coming today, and he doesn't like to see bruises that he didn't cause himself."

"Go up with her," the man orders.

Silent as a beetle I scuttle back into the kitchen. I wait for the girls to leave the room. When they are halfway up the stairs I steal back into the corridor and walk boldly into the room. The man

stands up, his face amazed. I recognize him from Kaja's description. The big guy with the red hair.

"Who the fuck are you?" he demands as he walks aggressively towards me. His accent is thick.

I put my hands up as if in surrender, one fist curled around the neck of the champagne bottle. "I'm just here for a bit of ass, mate. I even brought my own champagne."

His pale eyes flicker with uncertainty. He's obviously not the sharpest pencil in the box, but he doesn't stop moving towards me. When he gets close enough I brace myself, bend at the waist and ram my head into his stomach. Fuck. He's fit! It's like driving my head into a fucking concrete wall. Sparks of pain shoot up my neck and into my skull.

He stumbles, but manages to grab both my shoulders and shove hard, making me stagger backwards. I right myself, wheezing in and out. A look of amusement comes onto his face. Grinning and bending at the knees, he curls the fingers of both hands, motioning me to come forward.

He wants a little fun. A wrestling match.

I can hear the girls moving around upstairs. I don't know yet how many other people are up there so I don't have the time to indulge in his invitation. I put the champagne on the floor.

"No sense wasting good champagne," I say with a smile, but I'm so high on adrenalin my heart is skipping beats.

"None at all," he agrees. "Let the victor have it."

"May the best man win."

"That'll be me," he snarls, and moves, damn fast. So fast that I nearly miss seeing his change of tactic. He slides to the right, opposite to the direction he has been circling and throws a blow with his left hand and tries to hook my leg and hurl me to the ground. I sidestep, whirl and come face to face with him again.

He lunges.

I avoid one flying fist only to reel under the impact of another. My vision blurs. Fuck, he got me in the jaw, but I'm so pumped up on adrenaline I don't even feel the sting.

He charges like a bull straight into my stomach, but I'm prepared. I tighten my muscles, and he sees stars. I bring both my elbows down hard on his back, right between his shoulder blades. With a grunt of agony, he drops to the floor, rights himself up, and stands swaying. He stares at me panting hard, wanting blood.

We circle each other. Like animals. He brings his left fist up to fool me into thinking he is about to strike. The real blow waiting is his powerful right fist. I skip back and his flying knuckles miss me. I feel my hair ruffle with the force behind his blow, even as I land my own solid uppercut to his chin.

He sprays blood and saliva as the flesh around his mouth vibrates with the impact. He staggers back. My fist burns with pain, but I actually enjoy it. It helps banish the surreal feeling and makes me more focused.

With a look of stunned fury, he lurches towards me to try and bulldoze me to the ground, but I'm ready for him. I crouch to the floor. Rolling clear and stretching forward, I swipe the bottle off the floor. In one smooth action I stand and slam the bottle into the side of his head. Playtime is over, motherfucker.

The effect is instantaneous. His eyes dim and he starts going down. I catch his dead weight before it flops to the floor. I stab him with the tranquilizer and drag him behind the couch. I tuck his legs up so he is completely hidden.

Picking up the champagne bottle I go swiftly into the corridor. I start up the stairs and try the first door. It opens. Inside it is crammed full with four bunk beds. The girl who helped me and three other girls are huddled on one of the beds. I go in and shut the door.

"Who else is in this house?" I ask quietly.

The other girls are too terrified to speak, but the girl who helped downstairs stands up and whispers, "I'm not sure. Venus is next door with a client. The big boss is around too. They have brought a new girl in today. I think she is still in the last room."

"What does she look like?"

"I didn't see her. I just heard."

"I saw her," a girl with black hair says. "She is pretty with long hair the color of honey, and she is wearing a purple hat with a floppy flower on it."

That's my Sofia. There isn't another girl in London who'd wear something that ridiculous. "There's no one downstairs and the dogs are asleep so if you want you can run, but be quiet," I tell them.

The women look at each other, too frightened to save themselves. Only the girl with the bruises on her neck nods.

I go out and close the door. I avoid the next room. There is a bathroom on my right. I open the door to make sure it is empty. I don't need any nasty shocks, then I make for the last room.

To my surprise the door to the last room opens and a man walks out. The moment my eyes fall on him, blood slams so fast into my head it's like a baseball bat hitting a ball. I feel my whole body vibrate with tension as more rage than I've ever known pools in my gut. My right hand clenches into a violent wrap of bone, sinew and skin. Only one thought echoes in my mind. Over and over again.

Kill him! Kill him! Kill him!

Forty-seven

Jack

He lifts his eyes, sees me, and his head jerks back. It's a pure *what the fuck?-how the hell?-Oh shit!* moment.

Then our eyes lock and the moment hangs suspended, counted only in our heartbeats. They say that in times of extreme danger, the pathways between people open, they become connected, and there are no more secrets between them.

In that second, I see him in all his rotten glory: his narcissism, his arrogance, his sadistic cruelty, his dirty soul, his innate cowardice, and the demon sitting on his shoulder whispering dark thoughts.

And him?

He sees a man with hellfire blazing in his eyes and nothing to lose.

Then the pathways close and his tremendous opinion of himself takes over. His eyes snap to the champagne bottle in my hand. He schools his features into a taunting mask.

"How kind. You brought a bottle," he remarks, his voice smarmy, oily, repulsive.

"It seemed rude not to."

"I wonder about you, Jack. You don't look like a fool and yet you're on a fool's errand."

I unclench my balled up fist. "I've come for what's mine."

His eyes narrow. "She's *my* bitch, but for the right amount of money I can ... lend her to you."

"She's not yours. You sold her."

He makes a dismissive waving gesture with his right hand. "It was in a moment of weakness. A simple mistake that I rectified earlier this evening. Now she's mine again."

"You can't have her back." My voice is low. Calm.

His eyes glitter with something unholy. "I own her ass. She'll eat my shit if I tell her to."

I'm so repulsed, so horrified I can't even speak.

He thinks he sees a chink and pounces. "Why would a fine, upstanding man like you want a low life, dirty bitch like her? She's had more cocks inside her than you've had fancy dinners."

He's trying to get under my skin. The smug smile, calling me by my first name in that sardonic, superior tone, the fake concern for my wellbeing. This is passive-aggressive at its best. I'm not stupid enough to fall for it. I smile slowly. He thinks I can't play this game.

"I don't care how many cocks she's had inside her. From now on my big cock's the only one going into her."

He smiles, a dead, mirthless smile. "I know what. Let's ask her to choose. My big cock or … yours."

I shake my head. "This is not a democracy."

391

His lips tighten. "I don't think you realize who you are dealing with. You may have ..." he shrugs nonchalantly, "overpowered a couple of my men downstairs, but there are more coming. Every moment you stand here you are getting closer and closer to your own demise."

I shrug. "Let them come. I'm not leaving without Sofia."

"Then you'll leave in a black bin bag."

I lift my shoulder carelessly. "So be it."

He lifts his right hand and scratches his chest. What a fool. As if I'd buy that old card shark trick. His hand slips into his jacket, but before he can even aim his gun, I have pulled my knife out from the back of my waistband and have it ready to throw at him. He panics, turns, and tries to reenter the room he came out of.

Cat quick I throw my weapon. With impeccable aim it enters dead center into his left buttock, exactly where I wanted to plant it. He falls down and screams like a stuck pig.

I walk up to him, grab a handful of his greasy hair, and pull his head up.

"Fuck you," he spits. "You think you can get away with this? I'll hunt you down."

That's the problem with psychopaths. They just don't know when to stop, pull back, rethink the strategy, and maybe say sorry, I was wrong. Show a little respect to someone else. I shake my head in wonder. He's so fucking screwed and he doesn't know it. He actually thinks I'm just going to take Sofia and leave him here alive so he can then wreak his revenge at his own time.

"You'll be running for the rest of your life," he threatens wildly. Even at this late stage it doesn't cross his mind that he could have underestimated me. I could be a killer like him.

"Not that it'll help," I say, "but if you have any last minute prayers you

want to say, now might be the time." My voice is icy cold, deadly.

It hits him then. Finally, but damn, does it hit him! The swagger evaporates. His eyes bulge with the shocking knowledge that I'm not some lily livered, soft-touch, plastic surgeon that he can 'lend' his whore to. That I, a doctor tasked with saving lives, am prepared to kill in cold blood. That I've come to watch him die.

His face becomes a mask of raw terror. His hands start flailing, hitting out at my legs. He belly-crawls forward and tries to bite me. He has a split second of warning before I swing the bottle into the side of his skull. His head jerks so hard, it looks like it's coming off his neck.

Bright lights must be exploding across his vision right now. The screaming pain epic. His eyes are full of disbelief. He can't believe that it is over. *It can't be. I can't die on the filthy floor of one of my brothels. I'm still young.*

This can't be the end. He blinks rapidly, but no matter how hard he tries he can't clear his blurred vision. He struggles vainly against the rising blackness.

He gasps.

Everything is dimming, blurring, fading.

He reaches for me, his killer, blindly in a last act of clawing desperation. Then the world goes dark for him. The great Valdislav is no more. Gone to meet his maker, or those demons that surrounded him and whispered all their sadistic perversions.

I step over his body and go into the room. A part of my brain notes how chilly it is in there. A window is wide open and cold air blows in ruffling the curtains. My eyes go to the king size metal bed. I'm so sure I'll see her on it, that it is a shock to find it empty. My heart is beating so fast with fear I feel dizzy. I whip around looking for her. She'd better be here. I've killed the only man who might know her whereabouts.

Then I see her ... and the air leaves my lungs. My heart feels as if it is being torn into two halves. Fuck. I want to shake. I want to sob. My vision blurs as I lurch forward, hand outstretched, whimpering inside like a hurt animal.

Forty-eight

Jack

The cockroach has stripped her naked and squeezed her into a metal cage that is meant for nothing bigger than a medium sized dog. Her skin is blue, her hands open and limp, the way the dead keep theirs. When I shout her name she doesn't reply.

In a flash I get over to her.

Crouching down I touch her skin through the bars. Her blood is pulsing strongly. The door is secured with a padlock. I try to bend the metal and pry it open, but the metal is sturdy and won't budge. Blinded by tears of rage, I half-crawl and half-scramble over to the bastard's body.

I rifle his pockets, tearing impatiently at his expensive clothes. I find what I am looking for in his trouser pocket. Clutching the key in my trembling hands I stand over him. I thought I had seen the worst of humanity, but I have never met such a creature with such a black, pus-filled, moldy, walnut-sized heart.

Unable to help myself, I viciously kick at his despicable corpse before I rush back to the cage and open the door. She falls out and I see the needle mark in her arm instantly. I run my hands down her body. Nothing appears to be broken or hurt.

Going to the bed I rip the sheet off it and roll her in it. I shake her, rub her body, and kiss her cold cheek. I take my jacket off and wrap it around her mummy-wrapped body.

"Baby, it's me. Wake up," I urge.

Sofia

"Baby," he calls.

His voice sounds like it is coming through a long tunnel. Oh, he's so far away and I'm so cold. So freezing cold. Something hot touches my cheek. I force my eyes open.

"Jack," I whisper.

His mouth is like a furnace against my cheek. I try to wrap my arms around him, but how strange, I can't move my hands at all.

"I love you." My voice sounds like it has gone into the same tunnel to reach him. "Don't watch the videos."

I feel his hands slide under my neck and my knees as he scoops me up and carries me.

"I'm sorry. I promised I'd never take that shit again, but I had to break my promise." A tear slips out. "I had to choose between broken legs and a needle. I chose a shot in my arm. This is an old friend. I kinda like him, Jack. He makes all the hurt go away. He makes it so that nothing hurts anymore. Not even you."

"Shhh ..." he says.

My head hangs down. I should warn him about Valdislav. He could be coming any time. It is too dangerous. I open my mouth. I want to speak, but I can't. I want to keep my eyes open, but they won't stay open. I hear a voice. Is that Gorky? I should warn Jack about him. He is dangerous. He always carries a gun.

Jack

Oh fuck! The other guy that Kaja described, scar, black hair, dead eyes, has just suddenly appeared in the corridor. We face each other. Me, standing in the middle of the landing carrying Sofia and, at the end of it, him pointing a gun.

"Your boss is dead," I tell him.

"Put her down," he says, releasing the catch on his gun.

"Valdislav is gone. You can be the new king of all of this." I swivel my head to indicate the building around us. "All I want is her."

He doesn't blink. "Put the bitch down." There is absolutely no expression on his face, but I can tell that he doesn't know what the fuck is going on, and he dare not take my word for it that his boss is indeed dead.

"If you shoot me, you'll have the police crawling all over this place. Do you think I came here without precautions?" Behind Dead Eyes I see a shadow creeping up the stairs. Simply the way the man is moving tells me he's not a friend of Dead Eyes.

"Put her down or I'll shoot you in the head," Dead Eyes warns.

"Okay, okay, I'm putting her down." I just need to keep him talking for a little bit longer. Enough time for the shadow to creep up on him.

As I lay Sofia on the ground at my feet, I look up at him. "You don't believe your boss is dead? Go ahead and look behind me."

"Now, step away from her."

"Okay, okay, don't shoot," I say, as if I am really afraid of him.

A second later the shadow coming up the stairs digs the barrel of his gun into my enemy's back and says, "I've got no problem with you. Have you got a problem with me?"

I see the fear come into his black eyes. "I've got no problem with you either," he says.

"Then drop the gun and kick it away."

He drops his gun and kicks it.

"You all right?" the man asks me.

I nod. I don't know him from Adam and the only thing I can think of is that Noah sent him. Our strange impasse is suddenly broken by a man in his boxer shorts suddenly opening the bedroom door next to them. In that split second of confusion, Valdislav's man turns around and kicks the shadow's knees so he loses his balance, his hands jerking.

Expertly, Dead Eyes grabs the gun.

The man in his underwear starts screaming like a girl. In one smooth movement I reach into my sock, withdraw my knife and throw it. It's not for throwing. It's small and meant to be used up close; between the ribs directly into the heart.

It moves in an arc towards Dead Eyes. The aim has to be perfect, or we're dead. It pierces his neck, the impact throwing him backwards. He falls to the ground clutching his throat. I walk towards him. For a moment I stand watching him, gasping, eyes bulging, mad with pain.

I feel nothing. No remorse, no pity, no guilt. In fact, no point wasting a good knife, or leaving it behind as evidence. I bend down and pull the knife out. Blood gushes out of his body like a scarlet fountain. He dies from a bubbling neck wound. I move away even before his eyes become blank.

"Jesus Christ. What's going on here?" the man in the boxer shorts squeals in a terrified voice.

I look at him. His face is white. On the bed behind him there is a naked girl lying spread eagled. There are red welts all over her body.

I stretch my hand out and he jumps back in fear. He is too late though. I have cut his boxers and his wrinkled worm of a penis is hanging out. "Get out asshole," I tell him.

"My clothes," he says, covering his private parts with his hands.

"Get out you fucking sick bastard, or I'll cut your shriveled up, useless dick off."

He hesitates for less than a second. Then he runs, his pale body streaking down the stairs.

I look at the girl. "Get dressed and run. No one will come after you," I tell her.

The shadow has picked himself up and is watching me expressionlessly.

"Tell Noah, thanks," I say. I pass him by and pick my precious cargo up in my arms. I start down the stairs. The shadow follows me.

He opens the front door. It is freezing cold. There is another man waiting at the bottom of the steps. He nods at me as I come down the stairs. He goes into the house, closing the front door.

"Why is he going back in there?"

"He's part of the clean-up crew. One of the girls or the neighbors could call the police. They'll make sure the CCTV tapes are wiped clean and any evidence cleared away."

Another man comes towards us, nods at the shadow as he passes us.

Whatever. I'm not interested. I clutch Sofia tightly against my body. I need to get her to a hospital. I don't know what he has injected her with.

I place Sofia in the passenger seat, belt her up, and start the car. She mumbles something. I tell her to hold on. Then I call Lena and tell her that I've got Sofia and I'm taking her to the hospital. I give her the address then I end the call and concentrate on getting there.

Forty-nine

Sofia

I don't know what he injected me with, but it was so strong my eyes rolled back in my head, or maybe I'm just not used to it anymore. The night is a hazy blur of memories. I remember being cold. Shivering. Giving up. Wanting to die. Fading away. Getting lost in the soft dark.

Then being shaken awake. Jack. Noises. People screaming. Being carried out into the cold night. The stars in the sky. Feeling sick in the car. Jack talking to me in a crooning voice. Begging me to hang on.

"You're safe now. It's all going to be all right," he said again and again.

Then being carried into the hospital. Bright overhead lights. I recall the jarring sound of Jack shouting.

Noises, nurses. Being wheeled down a corridor. People peering down at me, calling me, 'love'. Kind words and hands, cold instruments.

Lena's swollen and red face hovering over mine. Kissing me, wetting my face with her tears, talking to me in Russian.

"Don't worry, I'm all right," I tried to tell her, but she cried even harder.

Eventually, it is all over. My body feels exhausted and heavy, and all I want to do is sleep. I close my eyes with the safe feeling of Jack's hand holding onto mine. In the night I wake up, suddenly, terrified. I raise my head.

"Where am I?" I gasp.

Jack leans forward. "Home. You're home, baby."

"Oh." I lean back on the soft pillows. How silly of me. Of course I recognize Jack's ceiling now.

"How do you feel?" he asks.

"Thirsty and ravenous for sugar," I reply.

He smiles. Slipping his hand under my body, he holds me up while he tucks two more pillows under my back. "I guessed you would," he says, taking a bar of chocolate from the bedside table. He tears the wrapper off and holds it out to me. I take it and watch him break open a can of Coke. He hands that to me too.

I take a sip. "Do you want a bite of my chocolate?"

He shakes his head.

All of a sudden I feel oddly shy. I drop my eyes and take a bite of the bar of chocolate.

He puts his finger under my chin. "Never hide from me, Sofia."

I swallow the chocolate and look into his eyes. "He didn't do anything to me," I blurt out in a rush.

I see relief cross his eyes. "I'm glad, but even if he had it wouldn't have changed a thing for me. Nothing can change the way I feel about you.

Nothing. You will always be mine and only mine."

I try to hold back the tears that burn at the back of my eyes. "I love you so much it hurts."

He uses his thumb to wipe away the tears that roll down my cheek. "My brave, brave Princess. There are no more monsters coming for you."

"What if he comes back?"

"He's a bit too dead to come back." His voice is hard.

My eyes widen. "What? You killed him?"

"I did."

I stare at him, horrified.

"To be perfectly honest I actually took great satisfaction doing it."

I cover my mouth with my hand. "Oh, Jack. What will happen to you now?"

He shrugs. "Nothing."

"Nothing? How can that be?"

"Trust me. I know what I'm doing."

"I really thought I'd never see you again."

"That was never going to happen, Princess. I would have gone to the end of the earth to find you."

"I was so afraid he would hurt you."

"Hurt me? I was willing to sell my soul to the devil for you."

"You do know that you're the most amazing man on earth, don't you?"

"I do," he says gravely, but his eyes are twinkling.

I put the chocolate down. "Jack?"

"What?"

"I'd like to have a shower. I feel grimy and my skin smells. I need to wash."

He helps me out of bed. My legs feel a bit shaky, but I'm all right. Before I can take the first step though, he sweeps me into his arms. I look up at him. "Oh, Jack. Not even in my dreams did I dare imagine I'd have a man like you."

"That's good because I never dreamed I'd get a beauty like you."

In the bathroom he runs the shower to fill it with steam, then sits at the edge of the bathtub and watches me brush my teeth and use the toilet. I turn to him. It is as if it's the first time I'm with him.

"Do you want to come in with me?" I ask, blushing.

He springs up and immediately begins to strip. "You won't believe how much, but I was trying to be patient," he says with a grin.

I pull my nightgown over my head and step into the shower.

The sensation of the water hitting my body, washing away the feel of Valdislav's hands on me as I lay on that dirty brothel floor, is wonderful. Jack shampoos my hair. He washes my body. When I am completely clean his mouth starts exploring me, starting at my ears.

Jack

https://www.youtube.com/watch?v=ZJ
L4UGSbeFg
(Save The Last Dance For Me)

Her scent intoxicates me and I experience a sudden and urgent need to take her forcefully. Prove to her and me that she is mine and only mine, but I don't indulge in that primitive craving.

No, I will savor every part of her slowly.

This whole night will not be enough for the kind of relishing I intend to do. I'm gonna lavish every inch of her body with Jack Irish. I linger at her breast, the soft flesh filling my hands, then my mouth. The nipples are little stones between my tongue and the roof of my mouth. Warm water beats down on my head. My resolve weakens. Fuck this woman has me in knots.

She is panting. Driving me insane. We both need it. I trail my mouth down to her stomach, her hips, her secret place. My tongue parts her and slips into that familiar sweet taste.

She cries out. I eat her out until her body shudders and quakes with an orgasm. I rest my head on her stomach.

"You came too quickly," I whisper.

Sofia

He stands. Looking down at me, he wraps his big, manly hands under my thighs, lifts me up, and enters me. I breathe a sigh of contentment. I'm home.

Finally.

Fifty

Jack

https://www.youtube.com/watch?v=43RCsADGE1Q
-Don't you know you're riding with kings?-

They come two days later. A middle-aged man with brilliantly green eyes, and two beefy officers in uniform. They keep their expressions carefully neutral.

"Jack Irish?" he says when I open the door.

"That's what they call me," I say calmly.

"Detective Chief Inspector Bradley. We need to ask you a few questions."

I step back and allow them into my home. I show them to the living room and stand with my arms crossed.

"Well?" I prompt.

Sofia walks into the room, her eyes darting from the men to me. I smile and wink at her. Her eyebrows rise with surprise.

"I'm going to have to ask you to leave the room, Madam, while we speak to Mr. Irish," the DCI says to her.

"She stays if she wants to," I say.

The DCI eyes me coldly. "I'm afraid this is a very serious matter, Mr. Irish. We are investigating a murder."

"Am I a suspect?"

He doesn't even have the grace to look uncomfortable. The way those in power seek to bully people that don't know their rights. "Your fingerprints were found at the murder scene and on what we believe is the murder weapon. If you cannot give me satisfactory answers to my questions I'm going to have to haul you in for questioning at the station."

I think of the champagne bottle. Probably with minute traces of the

cockroach's skin and blood. Fortunately, I'm already prepared for this scenario. Of course, they have my prints on their database from the time they hauled all of us off to the station after that massive fight outside The King's Maid Pub and fingerprinted us all.

"Do you mind if I make a quick phone call, DCI?" I say taking my phone out of my pocket.

He frowns, thinking I'm calling my lawyer.

I dial Blake's number. "His name is DCI Bradley," I say and end the call.

DCI Bradley's eyes narrow. Both his impassive escorts look at each other with surprise.

"I'm getting myself a drink. Anybody else want one?" I offer with a friendly smile.

DCI looks irritated. This interview is getting away from him. "No thank you," he says stiffly. "I don't drink on the job."

"Suit yourself. Do you want one, Princess?" I ask turning to Sofia.

"Okay," she says softly. I can see it's the last thing she wants, but she's just playing along.

I pour out a measure of sherry, and the silence is shattered by the sound of a cellphone ringing. It's quite an irritating bleep, actually. I put the bottle down. "You might want to take that, DCI," I say.

DCI Bradley gives me an odd look then he reaches into his jacket and pulls his phone out. He looks at the screen and his eyes widen. Turning his back on me he answers his phone.

"Yes, Sir ... No, Sir ... Right, Sir ... Perfectly clear, Sir. Thank you, Sir. Goodbye."

He turns around. His face is a picture. "Thank you for your time, Mr. Irish. I hope we haven't inconvenienced you too much."

"I'll show you out," I say with a smile.

"Let's go," he tells his men.

He nods politely at Sofia and we make our way to the front door. As he exits I call to him. He turns around. He's a good man, trying to do his job well.

"You can lay your head on the pillow tonight safe in the knowledge that for once the corruption in high places actually worked the way it should."

He nods and turns away. I close the door and Sofia is standing there. "What just happened?" she asks.

I take the three steps that separate us. "Blake is a member of the old Black Nobility. One phone call from him is all it takes to move mountains."

"So he made a call to the DCI's boss?"

"No, sweet darling, he made a call to someone who called the boss of the boss of the DCI."

She widens her eyes. "I didn't realize he was so powerful."

One day I'll tell her all about the secretive Blake Law Barrington. Today is

not the day. "I've got a question I want to ask you."

"What?" she asks, looking unbearably fuckable.

"Will you fucking marry me already?"

Fifty-one

Jack

https://www.youtube.com/watch?v=Ra
-Om7UMSJc
(Because Of You)

I stare at the breathtaking scene in front of me in awe.

"Well?" she asks beside me.

Snow falls onto my face as I turn and look at my beauty. Her face is framed in fur, her cheeks are rosy, and her eyes are sparkling like jewels. This is *my* woman. Sometimes, I still can't believe I've been given this wonderful being just for me.

"I'm actually speechless."

"That's a first," she says with a pretty giggle.

"True," I agree. All she would tell me for days was to book five days off because we were going on a longish trip. When I pressed her, she insisted it was a surprise. Even when I reminded her about the fate of her last surprise she looked at me impishly, but refused to reveal a thing.

I climbed aboard Guy's private jet, and I was the only fool who had no idea where we were going. Lena grinned at me and Guy just shrugged. All right for him. He knew exactly where he was going.

We landed in Moscow.

A two-hour helicopter ride and an hour long car journey brought us here. A hundred feet away from the edge of a huge Russian forest. Half-buried in the thick snow is a small house built from logs. It is as magical and enchanting as something plucked right out of a fairytale.

"This is where I come from," she says simply.

For someone who spent his childhood on the railway tracks and on a concrete playground, this place is beyond beautiful. "It's beautiful, Sofia."

"You always wanted to know about me and my childhood and here it is. This is the beginning of my story. I will tell you everything. Little by little."

I hold her around the waist. 'I would love that, my sweet Princess."

She wrinkles her nose. "I thought coming back here would be really hard. Even Lena was worried that it might be too traumatic, but it's not hard at all, and I'm glad I came back. It's time to put all those ghosts to rest."

"It was on a day like this that my father found a den full of bear cubs. The mother was dead so he brought them home. You cannot imagine how cute they were. I adored them." She smiles at the memory.

"What happened to them?"

She shakes her head. "I couldn't have kept them anyway, but they are part of the ghosts that must be left behind."

No wonder she doesn't want to talk about her childhood. A right monster her father was.

I take her thickly gloved hands in mine. "I cannot describe in words just how much it means to me that you brought me here. To where your life began. Thank you for being so brave."

"I'm not brave. You are," she says.

"We're both brave, then," I say and laugh. Not because anything is funny, but from pure happiness. She tilts her head and laughs with me. Nothing is funny. Everything is funny. Snowflakes fall into my mouth.

"Oh, Sofia, Sofia. How you have changed me. I'm your greatest masterpiece."

She shakes her head. "No, I'm your greatest masterpiece."

A movement to my right catches my eye and I turn to look. A tall, broad man has come out of the house. Next to me I hear her breath catch. For what seems like an eternity, the man and Sofia stare at each other. Then he turns away slowly, walks back into the house, and closes the front door. Never was there a more profound rejection than that simple action.

Tears glimmer in her eyes.

"Hey," I say softly.

"It's okay," she says swallowing the hurt. "He never wanted any of us."

"I'm so sorry, my love."

"It's okay. Lena once told me that my father gave us all a box of darkness to take with us into our lives, but I realize that in fact, that box of darkness is a gift. The day I met you that box became my gift. If he had not sent me on my journey I would never have found you."

"Oh, Sofia. I love, love, love you."

We make our way back to the waiting car. The snow in some places is so deep we sink into it up to our knees. Once she falls backwards and I yank her out, giggling like a child. I open the car door for her and she turns to take one last look. There is longing in her eyes. She still wants her father. After everything he has done there is no hate in her heart.

"Want to go and see him?" I ask softly.

She smiles. "No. Lena was right. There's nothing here for her or me. I was just taking one last look. I'll never come back here again."

Epilogue

Sofia

https://www.youtube.com/watch?v=NGFToiLtXro
Can't Take My Eyes Off of You.

"**B**aby, they're playing our song," Jack whispers in my ear.

I lean back into his hard body flirtatiously. "Since when is this song ours?"

He catches my waist and twirls me around as he has done a hundred times. "Ever since I saw your pretty pussy," he says.

"I could take that the wrong way, you know," I say sternly.

"I wish you would," he whispers, his breath warm, his lips trailing my cheek.

"Everybody is watching," I say.

427

"Fuck them. They're getting free food. What more do they want?"

"I don't think it's the done thing for the bride and groom to have sex on the dance floor during their first dance."

"Are you sure?"

"As you would say, abso-fucking-lutely."

He grins. "Are brides allowed to be so potty-mouthed?"

"Yeah."

"You're just making this up, aren't you?"

"No, it's in the handbook."

He smiles. "What handbook?"

"The bride's handbook."

He looks at me with that look. "Oh, *that* handbook. Have you read it from cover to cover yet?"

"No."

"Let me tell you what else is in that handbook."

"What?" I ask innocently.

"It's better if I show you," he says, and starts dragging me off the dance floor. People are laughing at us, but it is good-natured. I shrug and laugh too, and let myself be pulled away.

We get to the small room next to the reception and he tugs me into it and closes the door.

"You better make this worth my walk of shame back to the party."

"Baby, don't you worry. I'll make it worth every second of your walk of shame."

I don't even have time to laugh, because my great big skirt is flying up around my face, and my thigh is over his shoulder and his mouth. Oh, his mouth. Ah ...

Guy

Lena looks up at me, her eyes sparkling with happiness. This is her dream come true. We had everything and the only thing that was not right was

Sofia's unhappiness. Now Sofia has true love and our happiness is complete too.

When I gave Sofia away earlier I could hear Lena sobbing quietly. I stare into her face and suddenly it hits me. Oh, my God, I've seen that look before.

"You know, don't you?" she says.

I'm too choked up to speak. I just lift my angel off the ground and twirl her round and round while she throws her head back and laughs with sheer joy.

Yes, I'm going to be a father again.

Blake

https://www.youtube.com/watch?v=3JWTaaS7LdU
(I Will Always Love You)

I lean back in the chair to watch my wife dancing with my son, and my heart swells with pride. There is no woman more beautiful than my Lana. After all

these years she still makes the blood pound in my ears.

Memories flood into my head: the first time I saw her through gauze veils in that pretentious restaurant. She was wearing the tightest, shortest, sluttiest orange dress and hooker heels. Every man in the room was staring at her. I could never have imagined then the journey we would take together. The discoveries our bodies would make, the light she would shine into the darkness of my soul, the children we would bear together.

My eyes slide down to my son. How big he has become. I remember the first time I saw him like it was yesterday. Across the room in his mother's arms. The knowledge was like a thunderbolt. *My* son! My whole body tensed. Then I had to pretend like I didn't know he was mine.

I watch the intense expression on his face as he executes the steps he learned from me only a few days ago.

I'm still getting used to his Mohican hairstyle. I have to confess I'm not a fan, but to give him his due he carries it off well. An unwanted thought occurs to me. I wonder what his grandmother would have made of it. What the hell am I thinking?

Of course, my mother would have hated it.

Every time I think of her waiting like some starving vulture for Sorab's eighteenth birthday to come, fear fills my heart. I have done everything in my power to guide him in the right direction. It will be up to him. He will have to make the choice just as I had to.

I stand, walk over to them, and tap him on his shoulder. He looks up at me with a brilliant smile. My beautiful son.

"Do you mind if I cut in?" I ask.

He nods and releases his mother's hand. How formal. How grown up. What a bittersweet joy to watch him grow up.

He walks away and I turn towards Lana. She smiles at me. There is so much love in her eyes.

Ah, what a beautiful life this is.

THE END

Want to know more about Blake Law Barrington? Get him here ...

https://www.amazon.com/dp/B00M08LS6A
https://www.amazon.co.uk/dp/B00M08LS6A
https://www.amazon.com.au/dp/B00M08LS6A
https://www.amazon.ca/dp/B00M08LS6A

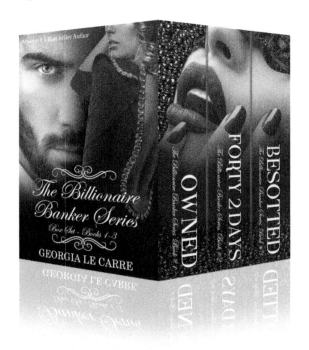

Want to know more about Guy and Lena? Start reading here...

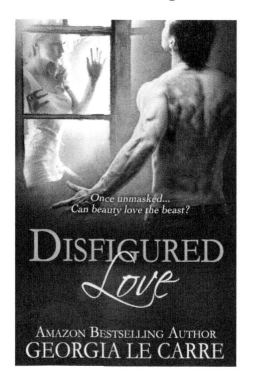

Disfigured Love

Georgia Le Carre

They must have the forbidden fruit, or paradise will not be paradise for them.

—Alexander Pushkin, *Eugene Onegin*

Once upon a time...

there lived a...

Hawke

Her eyes are a mutation. A beautiful mutation.

It was late when I finally stopped working and reached for the red envelope laid at the edge of the desk. I placed it in front of me, and simply stared at it, as if it held some great and frightening secret. In fact, its contents were prosaic and vulgar.

Some months ago, late one night, I had become so unbearably lonely and unhappy that I had actually *craved* the forgiving curves of a woman—any woman. So I went on the dark net, a place where all depravity is catered for and anything one could possibly wish for is in ready supply. I found myself a procurement agency... And signed up. In that brief moment I became everything I had detested in other men.

The intolerable loneliness of that fateful night no longer possessed me, but ever since then a red envelope had arrived once every two weeks. I'll admit, I did open the envelopes and look at the photos of those poor girls, modern day sex slaves. But even though each one was exquisitely beautiful, not once had I been even slightly tempted. I skimmed their fresh faces and nubile bodies without interest, sometimes with regret at my lapse in judgment, and other times marveling at the extent of my need. Never in my life had I paid for a woman and certainly not for an unwilling one.

I didn't even know why I still looked. Curiosity? Compulsion? But each time I stuffed those photos back into the envelope and threw them away, I became the unforgivable beast who condemned them to a fate worse than death.

With a sigh I tore the envelope open and slid the photographs out. My eyes

440

widened. What the fuck! I began to shake uncontrollably. The photographs fell from my nerveless hands and landed on my desk with a soft hiss.

This girl had cast her eyes out and looked *back* at me.

In a daze I picked up the photo and stared at her...ravenously. At her enormous translucent gray eyes, the small, perfectly formed nose, the flawlessly pale skin, the long lustrous blonde hair that spilled out and lay in curves around her full lips and slender neck.

There was something clean and 'new' about her, as if she had just come out of tissue paper. I reached for the other photo. Wearing a black bikini and red high heels, her arms at her sides, she stood in a bare room, the same one all the other girls had stood in. Leggy. Shining. Unlucky.

I turned the photo over.

Lena Seagull.

The bitter irony of it did not escape me. The hawk's prey is the seagull, after all. Her age and vital statistics were displayed in English, French, Arabic and Chinese. I let my eyes skim over them, although they were no longer of any importance. To my shock and horror I couldn't walk away from this one. No. Not this one.

Age: 18
Status: Certified Virgin
Height: 5'9"
Dress Size: 6-8-10
Bust: 34"
Waist: 24"
Hips: 35.5"
Shoe Size: 7
Hair: Blonde
Eyes: Dove Gray
Languages: Russian and English

My hand shook as my fingers traced the unsmiling outline of her beautiful face. How strange, but I yearned for the smell of her skin, the taste of those

plump lips. I had never known such irresistible desire before. I wanted her so bad it hurt. At that moment of longing I felt it, as if the photo was alive; I had an impression of a quiet, but terrible grief.

I snatched my hand away, as if burnt, and frowned at the photo. I must not fall under her spell. And yet, wasn't it already too late? The connection was instantaneous, beyond my control. I felt desperate to acquire her, brand her with my body. And make her mine. I turned to my computer screen and tapped in the secret code. The encrypted message was only one word long.

YES.

Almost instantly my phone rang. I snatched it and pressed the receiver to my ear.

'The auction will be held at two p.m. Friday,' a man's voice said in an Eastern European accent. 'And,' he continued, 'I must warn you. She will not be cheap. I believe there are already two Arab

443

princes who are also interested. What's your limit?'

'None,' I said instantly. In my mind she was already mine.

A pause. Then, '*Very* good.'

I terminated the call. There, it was done. I had sealed both our fates. My eyes seeking hers fell upon my own disfigured hand. Claw-like and ugly. And I heard again, as if it had happened yesterday, the sickeningly angry screech of metal against metal, the explosion that had strangely brought with it a blissful silence, and then the bitter smell of my own flesh burning, burning, burning: watching my skin bubble, crackle, glow and smoke. I had sizzled and cooked like a piece of steak on a fucking barbecue. I thought of the shimmering waves that rose from my flesh and shuddered.

My good hand moved upwards and stroked the raised scars on my face. The truth yawned like a black mouth: she would *never* come to love me. I was no

longer fit for love. A beauty such as she was stardust. I was destined only for the part of the lovestruck fool clutching vainly for the hem of her skirt as she blazed past. My hand jerked with the sudden pain blooming in my chest. It ate like acid. It was so horrendous that tears filled my eyes and a howl escaped from my mouth. The sound vibrated and echoed around the cavernous room like the cry of a wounded beast.

The sound shocked and disgusted me. I had never been weak. And I was not about to start now. I hardened my heart.

And so fucking what if she would never come to know my heart? I would have her, anyway. And think no more of it. She would be my pet. A human pet. To do with as I pleased. I laughed out loud. The sound rang out in the stillness. Unlike the sound of my anguish, which had throbbed with vital life, my laughter was empty and soulless. It disappeared into that deathly quiet castle and went to

lie softly on my two secrets as they lay
unconscious to the world.

Chapter 1

Lena Seagull

My name is not really Lena Seagull. Seagull is the nickname my father was given by those who knew him. While you were alive he would steal everything from you, and when you were dead he would steal even your eyeballs.

My first vivid memory is one of violence.

I was not yet five years old and I had disobeyed my father. I had refused to do something he wanted me to. I cannot remember what it was anymore, but it was something small and insignificant. Definitely unimportant. He did not get angry, he just nodded thoughtfully. He turned toward my mother. 'Catherine,' he said calmly. 'Put a pot of water on to boil.'

I remember my mother's white face and her frightened eyes clearly. She knew my father, you see. She hung a pot of water on the open fire of the stove.

He sat and smoked his pipe quietly. Behind me my sisters and brother huddled. There were seven of us then. I was the youngest. Two more would come after me.

'Has the water boiled yet?' my father asked every so often.

'No,' she said, her voice trembling with fear, and he nodded and carried on puffing on his pipe.

Eventually, she said, 'Yes. The water is ready.'

Two of my sisters began to sob quietly. My father carefully put his pipe down on the table and stood.

'Come here,' he called to my mother. There was no anger. Perhaps he even sighed.

But by now my mother's fear had communicated itself to me and I had begun to fidget, fret and hop from foot to foot in abject terror. I sobbed and cried out, 'I'm sorry. I'm very sorry. I will never again do such a thing.'

My father ignored me.

'Please, please, Papa,' I begged.

'Put the child on the chair,' he instructed.

My mother, with tears streaming down her cheeks, put me on the chair. Even then I think she already knew exactly what was about to happen because she smiled at me sadly, but with such love that I remember it to this day.

I stood up and clung desperately to my mother's legs. My father ordered my older sisters to hold me down. They obeyed him immediately.

Reluctantly, my mother dragged her feet back to my father.

With the dizzying speed of a striking snake he grabbed her hand and plunged it into the boiling water. My mother's eyes bulged and she opened her mouth to scream, but the only sound that came out was the choke that someone makes when they are trying to vomit. While she writhed and twisted like a cut snake in his grip, my father turned his beautiful eyes toward me. My father was an extremely handsome man—laughing gray eyes and blond hair.

The shock of witnessing my father's savagery toward my beloved mother was so total and so all encompassing that it silenced my screams and weighted me to my chair. I froze. For what seemed like eternity I could not move a single muscle. I could only sit, and stare, and breathe in and out, while the world inside my head spun violently out of control. And then I began to shriek. A single piercing wail of horror. My father pulled my mother's hand out of the pot and rushing her outside, plunged her blistering, steaming hand into the snow.

I ran out and stood watching them, icy wind caught in my throat. My father was gently stroking my mother's hair. Her face was ghostly white and her teeth were chattering uncontrollably. Then she turned to look at me and snapped them shut like a trap. I was never the same after that day.

I obeyed my father in all things.

*****

Once there were eleven of us in my family—my father, my mother, my seven sisters, my beloved twin brother Nikolai and me. We lived in a small log cabin at the edge of a forest in Russia. We had no electricity, no TV, no phones; water had to be fetched from a well; the local village store was miles away; and we had to use the outhouse even during the freezing winter months.

I didn't know it while I was growing up but we were a strange family. We never went on holidays and we kept ourselves to ourselves. We hardly saw the other village folk. And when we did see them we were forbidden to talk to them. If ever they spoke to us we had to nod politely and move quickly away.

Growing up we had no friends. No one ever came around. I do not remember a single instance when even a doctor was called to the house. My mother said that she gave birth to all her children without even the assistance of a midwife. On one occasion when my father was not around she even had to cut the umbilical cord herself.

I have a very clear memory of when she went into labor with my youngest sister. How she was in agony for hours and how my oldest sister, Anastasia, dared to beg my father to call the doctor, and how he refused with cold anger. Only Anastasia and Sofia, my second oldest sister, were allowed in the room with Mama so the rest of us had to wait outside in abject fear.

Many horrifying hours later my father came out triumphantly holding a baby wrapped in a blanket. He showed us the baby, red from head to toe. When we were allowed to go into the room to see my mother, I was shocked by the heavy stench of blood and stale sweat. My eyes were drawn to a bundle of blood-soaked sheets pushed hurriedly into the corner of the bedroom. My mother lay on the bed ashen with pain. She was so exhausted she could barely smile at us. Her legs had been tied together roughly with rope.

'Why are your legs bound, Mama?' I asked in a frightened whisper.

'The baby came out feet first,' she murmured. Her voice was so faint I had to lean close to her lips to hear it.

Mother had had a breech birth and she was so torn and damaged internally that my father had tied her legs together to stop her moving and encourage her body to heal faster. Even as a small child I understood that he never called a doctor even though she could have died. It was agonizing to watch her in the following days, but two weeks later the ropes came off and she hobbled back to the endless chores that consumed her life.

Other than those two scary weeks I can't remember any other time I saw my mother at rest. Ever. She was always flushed and slaving away over the open fire, cooking, baking, scrubbing, washing, ironing, canning fruit and vegetables for the winter, and in spring, summer and autumn tending to our garden.

My father did not work. He was a hunter. He often disappeared into the ghostly fir tree forest behind our home and came back with elk, faun, rabbits, chinchillas, beavers, wood grouse, geese and snow partridges. The liver and brains were always reserved for him—they were his favorite—some cheap cuts were kept for the family, and the rest of the meat and fur was sold.

When my father was at home he demanded absolute silence from us. No one cried, no one talked, no one laughed. We were like little silent robots going about our tasks. Come to think of it I never saw my sisters or brother cry.

The first time I saw my oldest sister, Anastasia, cry was when I was seven years old.

My mother was holding my sister's hands pressed within her own and whispering something to her and she was sobbing quietly.

'What's going on?' I whispered.

But nobody would tell me.

Chapter 2

It was midday and I was outside with my brother, sitting on a pile of wood logs watching him clean my father's boots when I heard a car pull up outside our house. For a moment neither of us moved. A car was an unheard of thing. Then I skidded off the logs in record time and we ran out front to look. Standing at the side of the house we saw the black Volga. I was instantly afraid. In my mother's stories black Volgas were always driven by bad men. Why was there a black Volga outside our house?

I thought of my sister crying in the kitchen.

Then like a miracle the clouds parted and golden rays of sun hit the metal of the car and gilded it with light. It had the effect of creating a halo. As if the car was a heavenly chariot. The front door of the chariot opened—a man's shoe emerged, and touched the dusty ground. I had never seen such a shiny shoe in all my life. Made of fine leather it had silver eyeholes and black laces. I can remember that shoe now. The shape of it, the stitching that held it together.

Another shoe appeared and a man I had never seen before unfolded himself out of the shining car. A short, hefty man with dark hair. He was wearing a black shirt, blue jeans and a leather coat. A thick gold chain hung around his neck. As I watched, another man got out of the passenger seat. He was dressed almost identically, down to the thick gold chain. Neither looked like he had descended from heaven. Both had swarthy, closed faces. They did not say anything or call out. They just stood next to the car with an air of expectancy.

Then our front door opened and my father stood framed in it. He moved aside and Anastasia appeared beside him dressed in her best clothes.

He turned to her and said, 'Come along then.'

She turned to face him. Her lips visibly trembled.

'Neither fur, nor feather,' my father said. It was the Russian way of saying good luck.

'Go to the devil,' my sister whispered tearfully. That was the acceptable Russian way of securing good luck.

'Anastasia,' I called, and my father turned his head and glared at me.

I froze where I stood, no further sounds passing my lips. Anastasia did not look at me; her lips were pressed firmly together. I knew that look. She was trying not to cry. She picked up a small bag—I found out later my mother had packed it for her while we were all asleep—and walked with my father toward the men. One of the men opened the back door and in the blink of an eye my sister slipped through. I remembered thinking how small and defenseless she looked once inside the car.

My father and the men exchanged a few words. Then an envelope exchanged hands. The men climbed into their shiny car and drove off with my sister in it. I felt confused and frightened. My brother slipped his hand into mine. His hand was rough with mud from cleaning my father's boots. My father, my brother and I stood and watched the car as it drove on the empty dirt road in a cloud of dust. While my father was still outside I ran into the kitchen through the back door where my mother was peeling potatoes.

'Where are they taking Anastasia, Mama?' I cried.

My mother put the knife and the potato down on the table and gestured for me to come nearer. Her eyes were bright with unshed tears and her cheeks were white, waxy and transparent. Bewildered and anxious I went to her. Immediately, she grabbed me and

hugged me so tightly her thin bones jagged into my flesh, and the breath was squeezed out of me. Her hands were freezing cold and the top of my shoulder where her chin was pressed in was becoming wet with her tears.

Abruptly, as if she had just remembered herself, she sniffed and put me away from her. 'Go and play with your dolls,' she said, wiping her eyes and cheeks on her sleeves.

'But where have they taken Anastasia?' I insisted. I could not understand where my sister had gone with the men.

'Your sister has a new life now,' she said, her voice hollow with despair, and picking up the knife and the half-peeled potato, resumed her task of making dinner.

'But where has she gone?' I persisted. I would never have dared insist with my father, but I knew I could with Mama.

My mother squeezed her eyes shut, the pupils twitching under their purple veined lids. 'I don't know,' she sobbed suddenly.

'What do you mean?' I asked.

My mother took a deep breath, her nostrils flaring out. With her eyes tightly shut and gripping the knife and potato so hard that her knuckles showed white she said, 'Anastasia has been sold. She will never be coming back. Best you go play with your dolls now.'

Her voice was unusually harsh, but that did not deter me. 'Sold?' I frowned. My child brain could not comprehend why my sister had to be sold. 'Why did we sell her, Mama?'

The knife clattered to the ground, the potato fell with a dull thud and rolled under the table. My mother began to rock. Violently. Like a person who has lost her mind. Her body tipping so far back on the stool I was afraid she would topple backwards. Harsh racking sobs came from her. No one would have believed that a woman that small and shriveled up could have inside her such a river of pain and anguish. It flowed out of her relentlessly, quickly and with shocking intensity.

'My daughter, my daughter,' she wailed. 'Oh, Lena, my Lena.'

I was so shocked to see the state my mother was in I didn't know what to do. I was used to seeing her cry, and I had come to accept her suffering as the way things were, but I had never seen her in this way, with her eyes unfocused and ugly sounds tearing out of her gaping mouth.

Sofia came running into the kitchen. Pushing me out of the way she grabbed my mother's hysterically swaying body and held it close to her body until the sobs were purged and she became as limp as a rag. Trembling, my mother separated from my sister.

She nodded a few times as if to indicate that she was all right and all was well again. Then she dropped to the floor and, on her hands and knees, found the knife and the potato as we stood, numb and watching. Wordlessly, she resumed peeling her potatoes. Her thin white face was tight with the effort of controlling her emotions.

My mother spent the whole day preparing elaborate dishes for our dinner that night. My sisters had set the table as if it was Christmas or Easter and we took our places silently. My sister's chair had been taken away and pushed up against the wall. I saw my mother glance at the chair and cover her mouth with her hand.

My father grabbed some schnapps glasses from the shelf and, filling them with vodka, took a glass to Mama She gazed sadly at the glass and dashed the contents down her throat. My father's eyes found hers and she swallowed hard to get the liquid down. I could hear the sound of her swallowing as clearly as I could hear my heartbeat.

Without Anastasia we began our feast. Except for my father, who ate heartily, everybody else hardly touched their food. We kept our eyes on our plates. Years of being with my father had taught us that both his 'up' and 'down' moods were equally dangerous and explosive times, when anything could happen.

'By Saint Nichols, eat,' my father roared.

We all ate. Even Mama.

My father laughed and called for more vodka. The second course was beet and beef bone soup. My father drank his soup in high spirits.

The main course was roast cock with root vegetables, and the potatoes that Mama had peeled that afternoon. I looked at my father. He seemed oblivious to our frightened faces, our furtive glances at him, and the horror on my mother's sunken face.

His ears red, and grinning as if he had won something wonderful, he sang, 'Ne uyesjai golubchick moi' (Don't go away, my little pigeon). He seemed an idiot then, but of course, that was only an illusion. My father was a bear killer. A thief of animal souls.

My father helped himself to fruit with shouts of extravagant joy. 'Slava Bogu!' (Glory be to God). The drunker and the louder he got, the more silent the table became.

Without warning he slammed his fist on the table. 'Why the fuck is everybody behaving as if this is a funeral?' he demanded. 'For sixteen years I fed that girl. Isn't it about time she contributed something towards the well-being of this family? We can't have any permanent drains on our family coffers.' My father squinted at us all. 'Is there anybody sitting at this table who disagrees with me?'

Nobody spoke.

His hand crashed down on the table again—plates jumped, a glass overturned. One of my sisters whimpered with fear. His blazing eyes swung around aggressively and landed on me. I realized then that everyone else had kept their heads lowered except me. I held his eyes. For a second something flashed in them but I was too young to understand what that might be.

Then he leaned forward, his entire attention on me. At that moment there was no one else in the room except him and me. I stared into his eyes and realized that nothing lurked there. His eyes were dead and soulless.

'Am I wrong, Lena?' he asked softly, with such menace that the atmosphere in the room changed. My father had found his target.

But for some strange reason I was not afraid. He was wrong to sell my sister. He should not even have sold the bear cubs after he shot their mother. I opened my mouth to tell him that, but under the table Nikolai took my hand and clenched it so hard, I cried out instead.

'Yes, yes, you are right,' my mother intervened suddenly. Her voice was high and shaky.

My father turned away from me and looked at her. She looked small and hunched, an unworthy opponent to the bear killer, but the horrible tension was broken. A grin crossed his face suddenly and he wagged a finger jovially at her. 'You do know that your daughter is an unbroken horse, don't you?'

'She is only young. She will learn,' my mother responded quickly. Her voice was firmer than I had ever heard it.

'She'd better. Unbroken horses are worthless to their owners.'

My mother did a rare thing. She maintained eye contact with him while his mood was uncertain. Maybe because she had been weak and let Anastasia be sold, that night she found it necessary to stand her ground and protect me from my father's wrath.

*****

We were all tucked up in bed that night when I awakened to the sound of someone at the front door. I hopped over my sisters' sleeping bodies and looked out of the window, and saw a sight I will never forget as long as I live. In the light of the moon my mother was naked and running away from the house. Her long dark hair was loose and streaming behind her. I could only stare at her ghostly white body in amazement. Then my father ran after her and caught her. Sobbing loudly she curled into a ball in his arms.

Gently, with great tenderness, he picked her up and carried her back into the house. I never understood the scene I had witnessed. Even now the memory makes me feel guilty as if I had seen something I shouldn't have. Something private that my mother would not have wanted me to see. I was always aware that she never wanted us to know that she loved my father to the exclusion of everything and everyone else. Even after everything he did. And even though she knew he planned to sell us all one by one.

After that strange feast, all talk of Anastasia was forbidden. The only person I could ever mention her name to was Nikolai and even then we spoke in whispers.

'Where do you think she is now?' I asked.

'I don't know. Maybe she is working for someone.'

'Doing what?'

'Accounting,' my brother said slowly. 'Rich people always need accountants.'

'But Anastasia is terrible at maths,' I countered.

My brother frowned. 'Maybe she is an English teacher like Mama was in Moscow before she met Papa.'

I nodded. That made sense. 'Yes, Mama did always say that Anastasia's English was the best. Do you think she is wearing fine clothes and living in a really grand house in Moscow?'

'Maybe.'

'Do you think she remembers us?'

'Of course.'

'Do you think she'll come back and see us?'

My brother's response was immediate and held a finality that I never forgot. 'No.'

Read More Here:

https://www.amazon.com/dp/B00QIQNWXW
https://www.amazon.co.uk/dp/B00QIQNWXW
https://www.amazon.ca/dp/B00QIQNWXW
https://www.amazon.com.au/dp/B00QIQNWXW

Coming Soon...

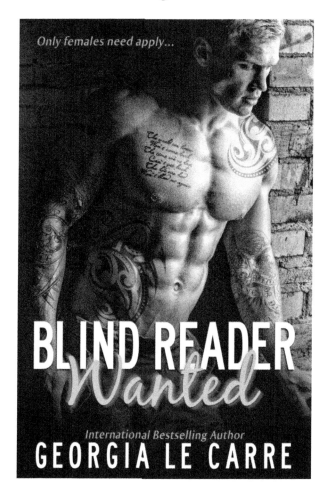

Only females need apply...

BLIND READER
Wanted

International Bestselling Author
GEORGIA LE CARRE

BLIND READER WANTED

(Only Females Need Apply)

Georgia Le Carre

One

Lara

I push open the heavy wooden door of Durango Fall's library and step into the still, hushed space. Other than my sculpting studio this is without a doubt my favorite place. I come here almost every day. I think I love the smell of old books mixed with pine floor cleaner and the lovely echo inside mostly empty, large stone buildings.

At this time of day there is usually no one around. I hear the water cooler gurgle in the left-hand corner of the room, and the lazy whirling sound the machinery inside the old heaters make. I shake the snow off my cap, take my thick gloves off and stuff them into my coat pockets. Swiping my white cane in smooth arcs in front of me, I take the twelve steps to the front desk.

Hannah Heinberger is usually on duty on Wednesday afternoons, but from her perfume, sage and roses, I know that Elaine is manning the desk today. They must have swapped shifts.

"Hey, Elaine," I greet as I reach her.

"Ooo ... just the person I wanted to see," she says.

I can tell immediately that she is bursting to tell me some piece of juicy gossip. It's funny how Elaine can always find salacious rumors in a town with a population of less than five hundred inhabitants. Notorious gossip or not she has a heart of gold and I cannot remember a time when we were not best friends.

I lay my left hand at the edge of the counter. Whatever the news is it has Elaine all fired up. She's almost bubbling over with excitement.

"What is it?" I ask curiously.

She leans forward, disturbing the air. Her breath warm on my cold cheeks.

"You'll never guess who came in here this morning," she cries triumphantly.

I keep my face straight. "Beyonce?"

"Fine. I just won't tell you, and you'll just miss the juiciest piece of information this town has heard in twenty years," she huffs, irritated that I've spoilt her surprise. I mean, who can she come up with who's better than Beyonce?

I grin. "Fine. I'm sure I'll hear from Emma Jean."

"I haven't told her yet," she says with great satisfaction.

"Elaine Crockett, I might miss the juiciest piece of information this town has heard in twenty years if you don't tell me, but you're going to burst if you don't spill the beans."

"Kit Carson," she blurts out instantly.

"Kit Carson," I echo, surprised. Well, well, this time she does have a juicy bit between her teeth.

Every small town has a loner, a mysterious, gruff, elusive, anti-social person who refuses to be part of the community. Kit Carson is this town's ghost. He lives on a large track of wooded land that he has converted into some kind of wolf sanctuary. Occasionally, he will drive into town in his pickup truck, but he won't make eye-contact, or speak to anyone other than to grunt.

I've heard he's a hulk: six feet seven inches tall and broad as a brick house, but he walks with a slight limp, and has a scarred face that nobody has actually got a good look at.

Funny thing about Kit Carson is he's turned the tables on our tiny town. We don't take kindly to outside folk. You can live within our midst for fifty years and still be considered an outsider. Kit Carson was not born and raised local, and coming on his own like that without knowing a soul in our town, he was just plain asking for trouble.

He came to Durango Falls when I was about seventeen years old. I'll be twenty-two in July. So he's been around for five years now, and even though our men folk have tried to extend the hand of friendship to him, he outright refuses to have anything to do with us except of the commercial kind.

Two years ago Casey Goodnight said she saw dog tags peep out of his shirt while he was paying for steel cables at the hardware store. Yessir, that gave the whole town something to gossip about for many mornings after.

With falsely sweet voices the good townfolk picked apart the man's "secret". He must have been dishonorably discharged from the army. It's pure shame that makes him avoid contact with the rest of humanity. He has no wife because what God fearing woman would want such a questionable man.

With time that particular piece of gossip morphed to -- he's murdered her.

People say they have heard the wolves howling on full moon nights while they were passing at the edge of his land.

The stories about him got weirder and weirder. Some of them are downright crazy. Serial killer stuff.

"Yup," Elaine says, "the man strode in here this morning bigger than a tree, stuck up a piece of paper on the Job's Board, and left. Not a word to anyone."

"Wow," I whisper. "What's he looking for?" I thought she would say foreman, or housekeeper.

She takes a deep breath. "Are you ready for this?"

"What?" I ask, inexplicably intrigued by the mystery of it all.

"Maybe it's better if I read it to you." I hear her rustling a bit with the paper. "Right. Here we are you." She pauses. "Blind Reader Wanted. Twice a week. Only females need apply. Kit Carson. And there is a phone number underneath."

I shut my open mouth. I couldn't have heard right.

"Did you say blind reader?"

"That's what it says here."

"What the hell is a blind reader?"

"A blind person who reads, I reckon."

I frown. "What on earth would he want a blind reader for?"

"Here's what I think," Elaine whispers. "I think he's ashamed of his scars. I think he doesn't want anybody seeing them." She catches a breath. "I think you should apply."

"What? No. Are you mad? That advert is just weird."

"Don't be silly. The man's not dangerous. He's just anti-social."

"Not dangerous! Aren't you the one who said, he killed his wife and buried her in the woods and the wolves are there so no one goes looking for her bones?"

She giggles. "Well, I was bored that afternoon. Don't you think it'll be fun?"

"You just want me to apply so you'd have all kinds of new gossip to spread around."

"What a thing to say? As if I'd do that to you. I'd apply if I were blind."

"No you wouldn't.

"Yes, I would," she insists.

"Since when?" I demand.

"If he'd only look at me, I'd do him. The body on the man. He's so hot I don't mind melting on him."

"Jesus, Elaine."

"Anyway, you should totally apply, Lara. I mean, I'll drive you there and sit in his living room and wait while you read for the man. So you'll be totally safe. It'll be fun. At the very least it'll be interesting. Please, Lara. Have a heart. I'm dying of boredom here."

"I knew it. You just want new gossip."

"Besides it'll do my eyes good. Man candy always does, especially the mysterious brooding kind."

I laugh. "I didn't know you were perving on him."

"So are you going to do it or not?"

"I don't know, Elaine. It's awkward."

"Look, if you don't apply. I'm going to poke my eyes out and apply myself," she growls.

I laugh. "I'll think about it."

"Call him now."

"Oh, hell."

Fast as lightning she dips her hand into my purse and extracts my mobile phone. Before I can protest I can hear her dialing.

"Elaine," I cry out as a ringing tone sounds. It echoes in the silence of the library.

Weird. I feel my heart suddenly become still. As if something important is about to happen. Elaine thrusts the phone into my hand. I take it and bring it to my ear and it feels as if I have waited my whole life for this moment, and finally it is here. I exhale the breath I'm holding.

"Mr. Carson?" I croak.

"Speaking." His voice is deep and smooth, but wary.

"My name is Lara Young and I'm ... um ... calling about the ... uh ... reading job. Can you tell me a bit more about it?"

"Are you blind?"

I blink with the directness of his question. "Well, I don't carry a white cane for fun."

"Fine. I'll go through the job spec when I see you. When are you able to come to my home?"

"Er ..."

"Tomorrow at two o'clock," Elaine whispers in my other ear.

"Tomorrow at two o'clock," I tell him.

"Do you know the address," he asks abruptly.

Elaine taps on my hand to indicate that she does. "Yes."

"Two o'clock," he says and rings off.

I put my mobile phone back into my purse.

"Isn't this exciting?" Elaine asks with a giggle.

Check out my FB page for the release date

https://www.facebook.com/georgia.lecarre

Thank you for reading everybody!

Please click on this link to receive news
of my latest releases and giveaways.
http://bit.ly/1oe9WdE

and remember

I **LOVE** hearing from readers so by all
means come and say hello here:
https://www.facebook.com/georgia.leca
rre